BETWEEN TWO

Club of Dominance 1

Becca Van

MENAGE EVERLASTING

Siren Publishing, Inc.
www.SirenPublishing.com

A SIREN PUBLISHING BOOK
IMPRINT: Ménage Everlasting

BETWEEN TWO DOMS
Copyright © 2013 by Becca Van

ISBN: 978-1-62242-950-9

First Printing: April 2013

Cover design by Harris Channing
All art and logo copyright © 2013 by Siren Publishing, Inc.

PUBLISHER
Siren Publishing, Inc.
www.SirenPublishing.com

BETWEEN TWO DOMS

Club of Dominance 1

BECCA VAN
Copyright © 2013

Chapter One

Charlene "Charlie" Seward stared at the large, brick, old-world, gothic-style building as she leaned against the side of her car, and she took a deep, steadying breath. She rubbed her sweaty palms down the sides of her black dress slacks and tried to calm her nerves.

You can do this, Charlie. You need this job. Does it really matter that you will be tending bar in a place like this?

With one final look down at her freshly ironed white blouse, she pushed off from her car and took the first step leading to the large, ornate wooden front doors. She gave a nervous smile when she noted the unique door knocker which look liked two whips intertwined with a cross of some sort in the middle, and prayed she was doing the right thing. Taking another fortifying breath, she grabbed the tail end of the wrought iron whip and knocked.

The sound of heavy footsteps approached from the other side of the door, and one of the doors was pulled open. The man standing at the entrance was tall and large, really tall and really large. And really sexy. *Get a grip, Charlie.*

"Um, hi." She shifted nervously and then offered her hand. "I'm Charlene Seward and I have a job interview with Mr. Pike."

"I'm Master Barry Winston." He took her hand but instead of shaking it just held it and studied her intently. He must have found whatever he was looking for because he smiled slightly and released her hand and then stepped back. "If you would come this way, Charlene."

Charlie followed him and felt trepidation crawl up over her body causing goose bumps to erupt over her skin. Club of Dominance was obviously very lucrative. The floor of the entrance was black marble, and the reception desk was set up with all the latest equipment. There were cameras on the ceiling and walls at intervals, and the hall was at least ten yards long. There were several doors along the hall, and another set of ornate double gothic doors stood closed at the other end to the hallway. Master Barry paused with his hand on the door and looked back at her over his shoulder with a grin, and then he opened the doors and stepped through.

The room he led her into was huge. The gleam of polished mahogany drew her eyes to the bar off to the far side of the room, and then she scanned the interior. There was a small dance floor in the middle of the large room and lots of small sitting areas with a two-seater sofas and armchairs to complete the arrangements. Each sitting area had potted plants and screens on two sides, creating a more intimate setting than actually was. The carpet beneath her feet was a deep rose color and very plush. Her shoes sank into it, and she wondered what it would feel like beneath her bare feet. She noticed there were open doorways and glass walls along one side of the great room, and she wondered what those rooms harbored. At the end of that long glass wall, there was another exit, which had a keypad on the wall to the side of it. Maybe the entrance to Mr. Pike's private rooms, she speculated.

Master Barry led her across to the bar, and it was only when she was a few feet away that she saw the dark-haired man sitting on one of the barstools at the far end. His hair gleamed healthily under the muted lighting and was long enough to be tied back. As he picked up a mug and sipped, his bicep bulged and rippled beneath the tight sleeve of his black cotton T-shirt. Charlie gulped as she took in his very muscular body. His legs were encased in tight black jeans, and he had such an air of confidence surrounding him, she felt intimidated. She met his piercing green gaze, and she quickly lowered her eyes to the floor.

"Boss," Master Barry said, "this is Charlene Seward. Charlene, this is Master Turner Pike, the owner and founder of the club."

Charlie took the two steps forward that would bring her closer to the intimidating owner and offered her hand. "I'm pleased to meet you Mis—Master Pike."

As Master Pike took her hand in his, he slid from his stool and rose to his feet. Charlie gulped and tried to step back, but the grip on her hand tightened slightly.

"The pleasure is mine, Charlene. And call me Master Turner or Sir." Master Turner's voice was a deep, gravelly bass and caused shivers to dance up her spine.

"Charlie," she stated, and cursed the higher pitch of her voice.

"Pardon?" Master Turner questioned.

"M—Most people call me Charlie."

"I'm not most people," Master Turner said in a confident voice and finally released her hand.

Charlie sighed with relief and finally looked back up into his face. If she hadn't seen the amusement in his eyes, she would have turned tail and run. Master Turner had obviously perfected keeping his face a mask of expressionless granite, and even though the man wasn't classically handsome, he was very good looking in his own right. His jaw was firm and slightly scruffy with the shadow of bristles, which only added to his ruggedly masculine appeal. He had a commanding presence. Charlie knew that even if he hadn't been ripped with muscle and a few inches over six feet, his confident air would have still drawn her to him.

"Take a seat, Charlene," Master Turner said firmly.

As she took her seat at the bar, Master Barry moved around to the other side and leaned a hip on the wooden edge.

"Would you like a drink, Charlene?" Master Barry drew her eyes.

He was just as intimidating as Master Turner if not more so. Master Barry had to be six foot five and he literally bulged with muscle. His light sandy-colored hair was cropped almost military short, and blue eyes pinned her in place.

"Water would be nice, thank you."

Master Barry must have liked her choice of drink because he smiled at her and winked then set about getting her a bottle of water. He was also wearing a close-fitting black T-shirt and black jeans.

"Why do you want to work at Club of Dominance?" Master Turner asked.

"I need a job and saw this one advertised in the paper."

"Have you lived in northern Oregon for long?"

"I was born in Tigard."

"Ah, a true local." Master Turner swept his gaze slowly down her body.

Charlie sat very still, though when she felt her nipples peak, she wanted to cross her arms over her chest to hide her reaction. His gaze lingered on her breasts and then connected with her eyes once more.

"Do you have a problem with nudity, Charlene?"

"Excuse me?" Charlie asked, totally taken aback at such an inappropriate question.

"If I hired you to work here, you would not only see nakedness but you would also see subs being whipped, fucked, restrained, caned, and probably whatever else you could imagine." He paused. "And maybe some things that have never even entered your mind."

Charlie should have realized to expect the unexpected in a place like this, especially from the owner and founder of Club of Dominance. She didn't have a problem with how other people lived their lives, but she didn't think she was into kink.

Then why did my clit begin to ache as soon as I heard these men's commanding voices? Shut up, Charlie!

"No, I don't have a problem with nudity."

As long as I'm not the one getting naked.

Master Turner tilted his head and eyed her blouse. Charlie knew what he was seeing. She wasn't comfortable displaying any part of her body and only ever left the top button undone. Charlie wasn't model thin, and being rather short seemed only to enhance her plumpness. When she had been growing up she had been teased mercilessly by the popular girls about her short, "fat" body and had become very self-conscious. So much so that she never wore anything to show off any part of her form. In fact she bought clothes a size or two larger to hide her abundant attributes. Since she couldn't change her body shape she'd decided she would choose her clothes and make sure that hardly any of her skin showed. Charlie had learned to be very meticulous when she bought clothes as that was the only way she seemed to be able to control how she looked.

"Why did you leave your last job, Charlene?"

Charlie bit her lip and lowered her gaze. He'd asked her the one question she hoped to avoid answering, but since it wouldn't be hard for him to find out "the why," if he called her old boss, she decided to be totally honest.

Raising her head, she looked him in the eye. "My last boss hit on me, so I quit."

Master Barry pushed the bottle of water he had placed on the bar closer to her.

Charlie grabbed the bottle and took a few sips. "It's in the past. It's not something I think about often, other than as the reason I need a job now. I quit, and I've moved on with my life." Her answer seemed to satisfy the men.

"How long have you been working in bars, Charlene?" Master Turner's voice drew her attention once more.

"I started when I was in college. I needed the money to help pay for my tuition and accommodation."

"You don't look old enough to have graduated," Master Barry said. "What did you major in?"

"Business management."

"Hmm." Master Turner rubbed his hand across his bristled chin. "How old are you, Charlene?"

"Twenty-four."

"All right. I'll give you a trial, but there are rules and regulations you need to adhere to. Master Barry, if you will?"

Master Barry leaned down and pulled something from a shelf beneath the bar. He placed the papers onto the smooth wood surface and pushed them toward her.

"You need to read our rules, and if you agree to them you will sign your name at the bottom. You will then sign the contract, but I need to know if you still want to work here after reading through our policies."

Charlie pulled the papers closer and began to read. They were so out there that she felt her eyes widen a few times, but throughout the guidelines, the words "safe, sane, and consensual" were used over and over. There was also a club safe word which was written in bold writing and underlined quite a few times. That word was "red." By the time Charlie had finished reading, her mind was spinning. *What the hell am I getting myself into?*

She looked up to see that Master Turner was watching her. His intent stare made her uneasy, but it also turned her on. Her cheeks felt warm and she hoped she wasn't blushing like a schoolgirl.

"Why did you want me to read this?" Charlie held up the rules to Club of Dominance.

"If you decided to accept the job, you need to know what the rules are. All the staff need to be aware of the club rules to keep our clients safe, as well as each other. I would hope that if any of our subs were in trouble and you were the only person aware of that, that you would call one of the dungeon monitors to intervene."

Okay, Charlie thought, that makes sense. "It says here that clothes must be acceptable to the environment. What does that mean?"

Master Turner looked her over once more, and Charlie nearly groaned aloud when his eyes lingered on her crotch. *Is he imagining what sort of underwear I have on?*

"What you're wearing definitely won't cut it for this club."

"What's wrong with my clothes?" Charlie asked indignantly.

The smile in Master Turner's eyes faded, and they became cold and hard. Charlie quickly lowered her gaze and stared at the floor.

"Look at me, Charlene," he demanded.

Charlie lifted her eyes to his, her heart beating rapidly against her chest. She hated to make anyone angry, and even though Master Turner didn't look incensed, he didn't look happy either.

"When you are in my club, you will wear the appropriate clothing." He looked over at Master Barry. "See if you can find something for Charlene to wear."

Master Barry gazed into her eyes and demanded, "Stand up, Charlene."

Charlie stood, her cheeks flaming with heat as he perused her body from the top of her head to her waist.

"Take five steps back."

Again she found herself obeying Master Barry's order and stood with her eyes lowered.

"Turn around, slowly."

Charlie turned and shifted on her feet uncomfortably as she felt the two sets of male eyes appraising her.

"Very good, sub, you may take your seat again." Master Barry moved out from behind the bar and walked across the large room to the door with the coded lock. Charlie watched as he disappeared behind that door until it closed behind him.

Who does he think he is, giving me orders and calling me a sub?

But that wasn't the question, she realized. What she really wanted to know was why she was obeying Master Barry and Master Turner. She wanted to know why her body liked the way they ordered her around.

Charlie drew in a ragged breath as cream leaked from her pussy onto her panties. If her body didn't stop, she would end up having wet trousers as well. She only hoped that if that happened the dampness wouldn't be noticeable.

She ordered her thoughts and asked the one question that didn't seem too dangerous to speak aloud. "Why did you call me that?"

"Sub? Because you are one."

She had seen the words "sub" and "Dom" in the rules, but she must not have understood the definitions, because she was *not* submissive.

Watching her reaction, Master Turner smiled slightly. "This club"—he waved his hand to encompass the great room—"is a place where people come to escape the stress of their lives. Not everyone is vanilla. There are a lot of people that need more in their sex lives to feel…fulfilled.

"Some of the men and women that come here are very high up on the corporate ladder of their careers, but when they are outside the workplace, they need to let go of that tight control so they can relax. Those people are called submissive or subs. And then there are people like Master Barry and I who like to be in control at all times."

"Doms," Charlie supplied.

"Yes. We like the rush of power knowing that we can control the pleasure of a sub, and therefore our own pleasure is heightened. In other words, we get off on controlling another person's pleasure. But rest assured that we only ever command someone who wants to be controlled, Charlene. Our club policy is always safety first and foremost. The mental well-being of any submissive is our priority, and all parties must agree to what is to take place. In other words, all parties need to consent."

Charlie thought about that. She understood where he was coming from. But he was still wrong. "I'm not a submissive."

The smile that crept across Master Turner's mouth could only be described as devilish. Charlene looked away quickly before her body got any more ideas. Her gaze fell on the contract, which she'd left on the bar. She scooped it up and flipped through the pages.

"Anyway, it doesn't matter," she said quickly. "I don't have to be submissive or dominant to work here, do I?"

"No, though if you do sign, I think you'll find that many of your coworkers have been drawn to this environment for a reason." He was still watching her closely, like he could see through her. "You are too."

She didn't want to argue about it. She couldn't think when he was here, and when Master Barry got back, it would only get worse. Her attention still on the paperwork, she asked, "Do you have a pen? I'm interested in the job."

Master Turner placed his hand over the pages and pressed them down to the bar. "I'm interested in you," he said deliberately.

"What?" She gasped. *I can't have heard that.*

"You *are* submissive," Master Turner said. "With your permission, I'd like to prove it."

Prove it how? Charlie realized that goose bumps had risen over her skin. She didn't believe his claim, but she couldn't deny that he had a strange power over her.

When she couldn't come up with a reply, Master Turner said calmly, "Or are you scared to find out?"

"Scared? What is there to be scared of?" Charlie ignored the tremor in her own voice. She let go of the papers and faced him squarely. "Okay, you have my permission. Show me."

"Remove your clothes, Charlene," Master Turner ordered.

"What? Why?" Charlie glared at him and crossed her arms over her chest. Suddenly fearful that this was part of the interview, she said, "My body or my clothing or the way I look doesn't have anything to do with how I do my job. My capabilities have nothing to do with my appearance."

"Agreed," Master Turner conceded with a nod of his head. "This has nothing to do with the job. This is about you, Charlene. However, if you do decide to play in my club as a guest, you must be able to abide by my rules. If I give an order, I expect it to be obeyed *immediately*."

Emotions warred in her chest. She hated being naked in front of anybody, much less a good-looking stranger. Yet something kept her from walking out the door. Master Turner's eyes held her gaze. He seemed to have no doubt that she would comply.

"You did say you'd let me show you," he reminded her. "Take off your clothes."

"Look, I don't know what you think you're—"

"Silence!" Master Turner rose from his stool and walked over to stand behind her. His large, warm hands landed on her shoulders, and a frisson of electricity tingled down her spine. "You aren't to question me. When a command is given, a submissive obeys."

"I'm not—"

"Did I give you permission to speak, Charlene?" he asked in that cold, controlling voice.

Geez, am I back in kindergarten? Why do I need permission to voice my opinion? I am not a child nor a submissive, damn it!

Then why are you doing as they tell you? Why aren't you fighting harder?

Shut up! Charlene snarled at her inner voice.

His hands moved from her shoulders down to the front of her blouse. When his fingers brushed against her skin as he deftly undid the second button on her shirt, she shivered with awareness. She wanted to push those large, masculine hands away, but she kept still as he slipped the plastic buttons through their holes, and when he pulled her tucked-in shirt from the waistband of her slacks, she didn't ask him to stop. The last button slipped loose, and he placed his palm against the flesh of her belly. His skin was warm, and she could feel calluses as he caressed her. After a moment he removed his hand and stepped back. From the corner of her eye she watched as he sat on his stool once more.

"Your skin is very soft and silky. Why do you hide your body away, Charlene? Are you ashamed of the way you look?"

Shit. How does he know how I feel about my body? He didn't even know her and he already had her pegged.

"No. Yes. I don't know."

"Which is it, sub? Whenever a Master asks you a question, you will answer honestly. Is that understood?"

"Yes."

"Yes, what?"

Charlie eyed him over, confused by his question.

"When you respond to a Master, you will address him as Master or Sir." His ensuing pause seemed to indicate that he expected Charlie to speak.

"Yes, Master Turner."

"Good girl. Now answer my question, Charlene."

"No, I don't like my body."

"Stand up and remove your clothes, sub."

Charlie couldn't believe she was doing it, but found herself obeying once again. She rose to her feet and stepped away from the bar. When her back connected with a large, solid object, she turned her head to look over her shoulder. Master Barry was standing behind her, and he placed a hand on her waist to steady her. He gave her a wink and moved to the side, where he stood watching her.

Her face felt like it was on fire, but Charlie was determined to follow Master Turner's command. She'd prove she wasn't the kind of woman who was easily intimidated, whatever else he might seem to believe. She tilted her chin, clenched her teeth, and pulled her shirt from her shoulders and off her arms. The cool air touched her skin, causing her to shiver and her nipples to harden even more. She looked down at her chest and cursed the white lace covering her breasts. When she had been dressing that morning she had debated on donning her black lace and bra panty set, but since the shirt she had chosen was white, she had decided on the same color for her underthings so her bra wouldn't show through the material. Now she wished she had chosen another color, because her nipples and areolas were visible through her bra. She hated having any part of her body on display because she didn't want to be ridiculed about her body shape, but she wasn't about to let this man know how much she hated how she looked. Maintaining control over what she wore was an intrinsic need she had developed since she was a young girl. Words could be so hurtful as she had learned from those popular girls at school, and she wasn't about to give anyone a reason to make disparaging comments about her person anymore. She was an adult, damn it, and she was the one to control whether anyone but herself got to see her body.

"The trousers, too."

Master Turner's voice drew her back to her task. She undid her slacks, lowered the zipper, and pushed them from her hips. The two men watching her inhaled audibly, almost gasping when her panties were revealed. The lacy panties were feminine and sexy and practically see-through. There wasn't much to them since they were a thong. She only hoped that Master Turner didn't ask her to turn around again. The last thing she wanted was for him and Master Barry to see the cellulite and dimples that graced her backside and legs.

"Remove your shoes and slacks, sub, and then come here."

Thank God I wore my slip-on sandals. At least I won't have to bend over and give them a sneak peek of my ass. But then Charlie realized that she was going to have to bend over after all. She needed to pick her slacks up off the floor. Otherwise they would end up wrinkled. Charlie did a quick bend and scooped her pants up with more speed than grace and straightened so fast she stumbled. After regaining her balance, she folded them carefully, giving the task more concentration than was necessary and keeping her eyes away from the two men watching her.

"What have you brought for Charlene to wear, Master Barry?" Master Turner asked.

Master Barry was such a big brute of a man, with muscles upon muscles, and he was really tall, too. His presence was just as commanding as Master Turner's and he was big all over. *Why do they both have to be Masters with that aura of self-confidence?* He was nearly as bad as Master Turner, not quite as domineering as the club owner, just a hell of a lot bigger.

Charlie clutched her pants to her chest and finally lifted her gaze. Both the Masters were perusing her nearly naked body. When Master Barry looked into her eyes, she felt as if she was drowning in those blue pools of his. She was aware that he had returned with a bundle of fabric that he now placed on the bar, but she couldn't look away from his face. Master Barry came so close to her she could feel the heat emanating from his body.

"Give me your pants, sub."

He held his hand out and waited. Charlie hesitantly gave him her slacks. She was hesitant because once he had them she wouldn't be able to use them to shield her body from view anymore and she wouldn't be able to put them back on whenever she wanted. Charlie followed him with her eyes as he placed her trousers on the top of the bar and then came back to her, once again.

"Take off your underwear, Charlene," Master Turner demanded, and Master Barry held out his hand, waiting for her to comply.

Charlie gulped and mentally cursed that the action had been audible. The two men would know how nervous they made her. Reaching up with trembling hands, she unhooked her bra and continued shrugging until the straps on her shoulders fell down her arms. Cupping her hands over her lace-covered breasts, moving her arms and shoulders again until the straps were drooping just below her elbows, she drew another deep breath, gathering her courage to meet Master Barry's eyes. Finally she removed her hands and let the bra fall. She caught one of the straps in her fingers and then passed it over to him.

"You are a good little sub, Charlene. Now lose the panties," Master Turner commanded.

Charlie had never felt so vulnerable in her life, nor had vulnerability ever come with so much arousal. She didn't understand why she was turned on by Master Turner and Master Barry giving her orders. Charlie was used to being dependent on only herself and she was a strong, opinionated woman. So why did these two men giving her orders and taking her choices away from her stir her dormant desires? But asking her to remove her panties was just too much for her.

She crossed her arms over her breasts, turned her head, and stared into Master Turner's green eyes. "No."

Master Turner stared at her long and hard, but this time Charlie vowed not to back down. She was going to redress and leave. Surely something else would come her way. Charlie didn't care what she did to earn money. As long as she could pay her bills and put food in her stomach she was happy, but she had morals too, and she wasn't about to circumvent her standards just for employment.

She turned back to Master Barry and snatched her bra from his hand. With quick efficiency she put her bra on and then skirted around him to the bar. She snatched her trousers from Master Barry's hand and pulled them on and then her shirt. As she buttoned up her blouse she walked back to her sandals and slipped her feet into them. She had expected Master Turner to kick up a fuss when she denied his last request, but he sat on the stool watching her stoically.

Charlie placed the last button into the hole and tucked her shirt into her pants and then walked toward Master Turner.

"I had heard that you were a good boss to work for, but I guess the rumors aren't true."

"Don't you think so?" Again Master Turner tilted his head slightly when he asked that question. He was studying her intently, as if he could see into her soul.

"I show up for an interview and you make me strip!"

"I told you that had nothing to do with the job." His attention strayed to the papers on the bar. "In fact…" He fell silent.

"In fact what?"

"About your attire," he said. Charlie realized he was changing the subject, but he pressed on before she could ask him what he'd been about to say. "All of my staff are expected to dress for the club. What you have on is fine for an office but not here." He indicated the pile of clothing Master Barry had brought. "You would be expected to wear a bustier or corset and a skirt which stops at mid-thigh."

"Isn't that sexist? Don't you know that you could be courting a lawsuit?"

"You read the club's rules. Anyone who enters the club must read and sign the forms. If you agree to stay and work here you will have to agree to sign the papers, too. As you are aware, this is not a normal place to work in. If," he added, "you still want to work here."

Now that Charlie had had a moment for it all to sink in, she didn't feel as annoyed with Master Turner ordering her to undress, nor did the crazy dress code bother her as much. The fact that her bosses would be so, well, bossy was more difficult to unpack. Though Master Turner had ordered her to undress, no one had fought her when she refused to take off her panties. They seemed to recognize that she had limits. Knowing that she could trust their restraint made her want to give up control to them. Was that crazy?

Master Turner had admitted he enjoyed being in charge and it turned him on. That made him a Dom. She'd been ordered around and it turned her on, which ought to make her a sub. But she wasn't submissive.

Am I?

Chapter Two

Turner eyed Charlene speculatively. This had to be the most interesting interview he'd conducted in his life, though he was no longer certain what he was interviewing Charlene for. She looked at him with her pretty brown eyes, a frown forming in the middle of her forehead, and finally asked the question he had been waiting for.

"What were you trying to prove by making me strip? It doesn't prove that I'm submissive." She hastily added, "Which I'm not."

"Aren't you, Charlene?" Turner asked and stepped closer to her. He heard her indrawn breath, and when she would have stepped back, he reached out and clasped her wrist.

"So when I commanded you to remove your clothes, you didn't become excited? Your nipples didn't harden and your pussy didn't become wet?"

Turner watched as she struggled to find a way to answer him, probably hoping to avoid the question. Charlene Seward wasn't very tall, standing at around five foot three, but she was quite pretty. Her blonde wavy hair framed her heart-shaped face and hung loosely down around her shoulders. The body she tried to hide was voluptuous and curvy with just the right amount of padding so that a man wouldn't be scared to give her some rough loving if he so desired. And desire her he did.

She was a natural submissive but she also had some backbone, which was just what he and Barry were looking for. They didn't want a woman kowtowing to them, or a slave twenty-four seven. No, they wanted a woman who had a mind of her own, who could think for herself and stand up to them when pushed too far. But the bedroom was another story. The bedroom was where he and Barry would have total control.

He glanced toward Barry and could see his co-owner was just as enthralled with the little sub as he was. Barry, along with Master Tank, was part owner of Club of Dominance, but Barry didn't like anybody knowing he was in partnership with him. Although Barry was just as domineering as he was, his longtime friend liked to keep his personal business just that, personal. Barry didn't want to be known as an owner like Turner was. He had wanted to earn respect from the Doms and subs that used the club, rather than automatically receive it because of his position or wealth. That sort of thing had never bothered Turner, although after they had first started Club of Dominance and he had seen how in awe of him some or their members were, especially some of the subs, he could understand Barry's reticence.

Turner had met Barry while they both worked for a security company and had become fast friends. They had known straight away that they were both dominant and had worked for another few years saving their hard-earned cash, with plans to one day open their own business. That dream had come to fruition ten years ago and neither of them had looked back since.

The club fulfilled the deep-seated desire they both craved for control and they were happy to have met so many nice people. They had made lifelong friends whom Turner knew he could call upon if the need ever arose, just as he and Barry expected them to call for help if they were in need.

But they needed a woman of their own. They had loved spending time with subs, training and disciplining them, but over the last twelve months they both had come to feel something was lacking. Turner had finally figured out that they were bored with different women and had stopped playing. Turner had just turned thirty-five and Barry was thirty-three. Both felt it was time that they started looking for a woman to settle down with. Someone they could both love and cherish and maybe start a family with.

Could Charlene be that woman? If she decided to stay and tend bar, he and Barry were going to want to explore her submissive side. She was a beautiful woman and he wanted to be able to act on the attraction he felt for her. He wasn't sure he wanted her as an employee though. Much though they needed a bartender, and as well qualified as Charlene was, it would only muddy the waters if she worked for them.

When she opened her mouth to finally answer him, Turner cut her off. "Don't try and lie to me, Charlene. I know an aroused woman when I see one."

"Just because my body reacted doesn't mean I'm submissive. You and Barry are very handsome, muscular men. What woman wouldn't be a little turned on by such masculinity?"

Turner hid the smile trying to form on his mouth and stepped away from her again. He nodded to Barry to do the same and they both sat on the barstools once more.

"Come here, Charlene," Barry instructed and pointed to the spot between his spread thighs.

Charlene moved immediately and then scowled up at Barry when she realized what she had done.

"You are definitely a sub, baby." Barry reached up and threaded his fingers through Charlene's hair, tilting her head back and fisting her tresses in a firm grip. "Just look at the way you respond to my commands. Look at the way your body reacts."

Turner studied her body's reaction. Her nipples were hard little points, visible beneath the material of her shirt, and she pressed her thighs together as if trying to relieve the ache between her legs. Blood rushed to her face and tinted the skin on her cheeks a pink hue. When Barry lowered his head toward her, bringing his lips closer to hers, Charlene's parted as if waiting for his kiss. Her breath panted from between those lush cupid bows and her eyelids began to slide closed.

Oh yes, she was absolutely perfect, and if she stayed he and Barry were going to do their damnedest to get her into their bed. But first they would need to introduce her to their dominant side. There was no way in hell he was going to deceive her. She needed to know up front who and what she was dealing with.

Barry finally brushed his lips over hers and Turner heard the small feminine whimper she tried to hold back, but she didn't stand a chance against two very experienced Doms. His friend deepened the kiss and opened his mouth over hers, bringing his tongue into play. Turner watched their tongues dancing and tangling together, and the sexual tension in the room was so thick he could virtually see it. Watching Barry have his first taste of Charlene made his cock fill rapidly with blood until it was so engorged it was painful. His balls were aching and hard, wanting release so bad he was afraid for the first time in years that he might come in his pants.

Barry gripped Charlene's hips and slowly walked her toward Turner while keeping her mouth occupied. When her back bumped against Turner's knee, his friend finally slowed the kiss and then stopped. Charlene was panting for breath, as was Barry.

Normally Turner was the type of man who took what he wanted and damn the consequences, but this time he was going to have to be careful not to push their little sub too far or they would send her running. Turner knew that, if she would allow it, the three of them could have something very special. But as with all good things, they were going to have to work for what they wanted.

He watched her in the mirror behind and off the side of the bar, which gave him a great view of her face, since her back was to him. Charlene reached up and touched the tips of her fingers to her lips and stared at Barry as if he had two heads. Turner would have loved to know what was going through her pretty little head right at that moment. When she moved again and bumped into his knee, she seemed to remember that he was there watching. *Was she so wrapped up in Barry she forgot about me?*

"Sorry," she mumbled and tried to step around him.

Turner wasn't going to allow that. He wanted a taste of that sweet mouth, too. Leaning close, he wrapped and arm around her middle and lifted her from the floor. She gave a squeak of startled surprise which immediately stopped when he plopped her ass down on his lap. He shifted her so that she was sitting across him with both her legs dangling over one of his. His arm still around her waist to prevent her from moving, he slid a hand beneath her hair to cup the back of her neck.

"What are you—"

Turner slammed his mouth over hers, cutting her off. He groaned at the first contact of their lips and sweetness of her mouth. She tasted so damn fresh and innocent. He knew he would never get enough. He thrust his tongue into her mouth and swept it around, tasting everything she had to give. Removing his hands from her middle and neck, he smoothed them down her arms and brought her wrists together behind her back. He gently shackled them into one of his large hands and gripped her hip with the other. She moaned into his mouth and arched her chest forward until her breasts were pillowed against his chest.

Oh yes! Abso-fucking-lutely perfect.

Turner wound the kiss down and then sipped at her lips a few times until she gave a breathy sigh and he lifted his head. Her eyes were glazed with passion, her eyelids heavy as if weighted, and her cheeks flushed. Yes, she was definitely worth pursuing. He gently released her wrists and rubbed his hands up and down her arms.

Charlene stiffened in his arms and sat straighter on his lap. She placed her palms against his chest and pushed. Turner let her go and didn't try to stop her when she slid off his legs. She stumbled slightly as her feet landed on the ground, and Barry quickly reached out to steady her. She spun away from his touch and walked a few steps from the bar, putting a little distance between them before turning back to glare at both of them.

She crossed her arms over her chest defensively but contradicted that action by thrusting her beautiful little chin in the air and scowling.

"Why the hell did you do that?"

"Because you are so damn sexy and we couldn't resist," Barry answered with a smile and then winked, which only made her scowl all the more.

"Are you playing with me?"

"No," Turner replied, drawing her attention. "You are an innate submissive, Charlene, and such a stunning woman. What dominant man could resist taking a taste of those sweet lips?"

Charlene didn't seem to have anything to say to that.

"Do you want the job, Charlene?"

Her scowl faded and Turner could see her weighing the pros and cons.

"Yes, I want the job," she said, and then held up a finger when Turner was about to speak. "But I don't want any man coming on to me or groping me. I just left one asshole of a boss because he couldn't keep his hands to himself. I don't need to jump from the frying pan into the fire. Did you expect me to put out just to secure this job?"

"No!" He and Barry immediately answered her question with a yell.

"Rest assured that we will *never* allow anyone to touch you, Charlene."

"Anyone? Even you?"

He tapped the paperwork still lying on the bar. "If it were up to me, I'd rip all this up before I could sign it."

"I thought you were offering me the job," she squeaked. Though she looked hurt, she didn't seem surprised.

Oh, baby. You don't have much faith in yourself, do you?

"We are," Barry rushed to assure her. "But there's something we want more."

He paused and met Turner's eye. Turner gave a tiny nod. As usual, he and his friend were on the same wavelength.

"We want to help you explore your submissive side," Barry said to Charlie. "This is something separate from your work for us. It's something for you."

"We would never force you to do anything you don't want to do." Turner wondered if she would pick up on his play on words. *But that doesn't mean we won't explore your wants and needs and your submissive tendencies. We will give you what you need, Charlene. Not just what you think you want.*

She stared at him with a frown and nibbled on her lip. What he'd said he'd meant, but he knew how to read a woman and knew when she wanted to be touched. He intended to push her boundaries and see how far she would let them lead her. Turner couldn't wait to begin courting her. And if she agreed to play, he and Barry were going to introduce her to the lifestyle of Dominants and submissives.

Now to see if she agrees.

"What would I have to do?" she asked in a small voice. "You wouldn't…I mean, you wouldn't hurt me, would you?"

"Never," Barry assured her.

"Club of Dominance is orientated toward the D/s part of BDSM," Turner said. "I have no interest in the sadomasochistic side of the lifestyle and I don't allow that sort of thing in his club. Barry and I are into bondage, spanking, light whipping, and sex toys. I allow wax play and cupping, but there is never to be any real hard pain in my club."

He'd watched Charlie's eyes widen as he explained. "I don't know what…"

"Don't worry about it. Choosing the type of play is our job," Barry said.

"You don't have to worry about other Doms here, either," Turner said. "This is an informal agreement, but it's an exclusive one. You may be asked to help other Doms by handing over their equipment, which we would allow, and we expect you to answer and obey those demands with respect. But rest assured that no sexual demands will be made from other Dominants. That will be an exclusivity only Master Barry and I will have."

He could imagine the kind of fears rolling through Charlie's mind, but he was particular about behavior in his club. If any of the visiting Doms pushed beyond his rules, then they were banned. They all had to read the club rules and sign the consent forms to show they understood his policies. He had dungeon monitors in the club all night every night observing scenes for the protection of the subs. The monitors were usually Doms themselves and had learned to read if a sub was into a scene or not, and they would stop the action immediately if the sub were in danger.

That went for the Doms as well. The monitors would step in if a sub was topping from the bottom, and either take over the play or send another more experienced Dom into the scene. Subs had to learn that they weren't in control, since the reason they attended his venue was to give up their power, so Turner made sure their desires were met.

Of course, now Charlene knew these rules, too, but she had yet to sign the forms or agree to their proposal. If she worked for them but wouldn't play with them, Turner would have to undergo the torture of working beside her without touching her. Just as bad, Charlie might never learn what pleasure her body was capable of giving her in skilled hands like his and Barry's.

She was biting her lip again as she contemplated the suggestion. "So if it doesn't work out, I won't have to quit, right?"

"Not at all," Turner said. "The job is separate from whatever the three of us agree to."

She took a fortifying breath and nodded firmly. "Okay. I want to…I want to try. And I want the job."

Barry picked up the papers Charlene had left on the bar and turned back toward her. "Sign these, baby."

Charlene took a hesitant step forward and then pushed her shoulders back and walked with gracefully casual calm. Turner doubted that was what she felt though. He saw all the signs she was trying to hide. Her mouth was pulled tight and her shoulders were too tense, but she picked up the pen lying on the bar, snatched the papers from Barry, and signed on the dotted line.

"Good." The tension drained from Turner's muscles. Until she signed those papers he still hadn't been too sure she would accept the job. He picked up the skirt and corset Barry had retrieved from the closet where he kept spare clothes. "I want you back here at seven sharp tomorrow night dressed in this outfit. You may wear a coat for protection from the cold, but when you enter the club, you are to leave it with the receptionist, who will hang it in the closet for you. You will be working with Barry until you become comfortable with where everything is."

And so no other Doms can lure you away.

Turner knew that the other men were going to be intrigued by her. Charlene was a paradox. One minute she was feisty and the next sweet and innocent, and as far as Turner could see it wasn't an act. He couldn't wait to unravel her layers and find out who the real woman was and what made her tick.

Charlene held up the skirt and then the corset and eyed them with wide eyes. She glanced toward him and then blushed when she caught him watching her. She was definitely shy. He wondered if she would have a problem displaying her body in public. From what he had seen earlier he thought she would, but he'd also seen the pulse beating hard and fast at the base of her throat. Even though she had been nervous and a little intimidated by him and Barry, she had also been very aroused. Turner decided to push her a little more.

"And, Charlene, as my submissive, you aren't to wear panties or a bra."

Charlene's shocked little gasp amused him greatly. After a moment of silence, she finally lowered the outfit and let it dangle from one hand as she looked at him and then Barry. "Fine, I'll wear your stupid outfit."

Turner bit his tongue to hide his smile. Her statement had been said with resignation, but there was a definite sparkle in her eyes. It looked like their little sub was excited about wearing such different clothes. He wondered why she tried to hide such a beautiful curvy body. When he and Barry were closer to her, he intended to take her shopping. There would be no shapeless shirts or slacks for her. No, he would make sure she had feminine things which showcased her stunning voluptuous figure. He glanced toward his friend and saw the glimmer of humor in his eyes, too. They were always attuned to each other, so he knew that Barry had caught on to the excitement she had shown. Showing her how sexy she was and how much gratification they could give her was going to be a pleasure.

Charlene turned away from them and walked toward the double doors leading to the hallway. Barry gave him a wink as Turner turned to follow her. He moved around her quickly and opened the doors for her and then gestured for her to precede him. Biting back another smile at her harrumph, he walked at her side until they were at the entrance.

Turner took her hand in his and held it much longer than necessary and watched as goose bumps raced up her arm. *Oh yes, little sub, you are definitely feeling the attraction. I can't wait to tap into all the passion and set it free.*

"It was nice meeting you, Charlene. Drive carefully and we'll see you tomorrow night." Turner opened the door.

Charlene snatched her hand from his, gave him one more glare, and hurried down the steps to her car. As she got into the driver's seat and drove away, she gave him surreptitious glances.

He went back inside to speak with Barry. They had some planning to do, and although they would have to take care not to push little Charlene Seward too far, push her they would.

Barry was waiting for him and gave him a smile. "She could be the one, couldn't she?"

"Yes, I think she just might be."

"You know she's going to fight us every step of the way." Barry's smile widened.

"Yes, I think she'll lead us on a merry chase." Turner smiled, too. "Little Miss Charlene doesn't even know how submissive she is."

"Yeah, I got that. We've planted the seed though. Want to place a wager that she comes in here tomorrow tired after a sleepless night?"

"You know I don't gamble, Barry. Besides, that's a no-brainer. I don't place bets when I know the outcome."

"Man, I'm as hard as steel right now," Barry groaned and shifted on his seat. "I don't know how I'm gonna get through tonight without her here. God, some of the subs who attend the club are so damn needy, they're more like slaves. Not that there is anything wrong with that, but that's not what I'm looking for. I just wish they didn't come after you and me so much. I'm getting sick of being alone though, Turner. We need to convince Charlie we are what she needs."

"I agree with you, Barry. I like her nickname and nearly slipped up by calling her that a few times, but I just couldn't help myself when she practically demanded we call her by it."

"Shit, it is going to be a long thirty-odd hours."

"Yes it is, my friend. But as the saying goes, 'patience is a virtue.'"

"Yeah, but I don't like her not being here where we can keep an eye on her. If she was here under our protection I could be as patient as a snail, but since she's not I'm on damned pins."

"As am I, Barry." Turner sighed and slapped his friend on the shoulder. "Let's get to work. If we keep ourselves occupied then the time will go faster."

"Do you think we'll be able to convince her to move in here? We can give her one of the spare rooms."

"One step at a time, my friend." Although Turner was spouting out aphorisms, he was just as eager as Barry. Turner was very easygoing and patient and Barry the eager beaver, but this time he was just as zealous as his friend. He tamped down his thoughts and headed toward his office. Tomorrow night would be upon them before they knew it.

God, I hope so!

Chapter Three

Charlie eyed herself in the mirror. If she wasn't so plump, she might have looked hot in the outfit Master Turner and Master Barry had given her to wear. When she studied her body, all she saw was bulges and cellulite. She wanted to rip the corset and skirt off and throw them away, but she needed this job and couldn't afford to do anything which would get her thrown out of the club before she even started. And even though she wasn't sure the clothes suited her, she was secretly glad the two Masters had ordered her to wear them.

What is up with that? God, Charlie, since when do you like being told what to do or wear?

She could hardly believe how she had reacted when the two Doms had started making demands and giving her orders. Her traitorous body had come to life and lit up for the first time in like forever. She never would have suspected that she liked being told what to do. Since being a teenager Charlie had learned to control nearly every aspect of her life, especially what clothes she wore as she tried to hide as much skin as she could. She glanced down at her legs. As far as she was concerned they were her best feature other than her hair.

The first taste of the Dom/sub side of BDSM had been a rude awakening. She shivered with desire as she remembered Masters Barry and Turner's low, commanding voices telling her what to do. Who would have thought that being told what to do could be such a turn-on? Another shudder ripped through her body at the thought of giving up all control to those two men. She was filled with nervous excitement but also trepidation. *What are they going to do to me?*

Don't worry about that now, Charlie. You need to get going.

Slipping her feet into her red heels and giving one last critical look at herself, she sighed and turned away from the mirror. She hoped no one checked on the underwear rule either, because Charlie didn't feel comfortable not wearing panties. Not having a bra was no problem since the corset kept her breasts in place and she wouldn't be self-conscious about them jiggling everywhere. But to go without her undies was just not her style.

Nothing was going to change, and there was nothing she could do about her fat body.

She could hear her mother's voice in her head whenever she glanced in a mirror. The disparaging comments had started when she wasn't even in her teens and had continued until she was an adult. Charlie hardly spoke to her mom anymore because all she heard was derogatory aphorisms.

Your ass is the size of the back of a bus, Charlene. You need to stop eating so much and exercise more. You should be more like your sister, Charity. She knows how to take care of her body.

No matter what Charlie had done over the years to lose the extra pounds, nothing had ever worked, so she had resigned herself to always being short and dumpy. But what had hurt the most was whenever Charlie had been interested in the opposite sex growing up, Charity had always seemed to know and would end up dating the boy she had been pining after. In the end Charlie had given up trying to please anyone but herself, but she still had low self-esteem where her body was concerned.

Well, Charlie, there is nothing you can do about it now, so take a deep breath and get your fat ass moving or you're going to be late on your first night.

Half an hour later, Charlie pulled up at the side of the club where staff were allowed to park and turned off her ignition. It was still early, but the parking lot was nearly full. Master Turner must have a hell of a lot of people working for him. Or maybe the members parked in the staff lot as well. Yeah, that was probably it. She still had so much to learn, but she gave a little shrug, confident that her work wouldn't be in question. What worried her most was how she was going to handle seeing the stuff that went on inside the club. She hoped she didn't spend the whole night with a bright red face.

Taking a few deep, calming breaths, Charlie grabbed her purse, got out, locked the car, and made her way toward the front entrance. By the time she was on the top landing, her legs were quivering with nervousness and her palms were sweaty, but she was used to hiding her feelings from living with her mom and sister most of her life. Charity's tongue had often become more malicious if Charlie showed that her sister's words affected her, but at this moment she thanked her family for the lesson.

Seeing that one of the large doors was standing open, Charlie entered the foyer and walked over to the reception area, where a man and woman were working and talking behind the counter. She felt even more self-aware when she saw how petite and slim the woman was, but when she looked up at Charlie a wide, welcoming smile crossed her face. The man gave her the once-over and then smiled, but he was so damn big and muscular that his size was intimidating.

"Hi, you must be Charlene. I'm Aurora and this big brute is Master Tank."

"Hi." She smiled nervously. "Please call me Charlie."

Master Tank came out from behind the counter and smiled down at her. "Let me help you with your coat, Charlie."

"Thanks."

"No problem, sweetie. Aurora, why don't you take Charlie to the lockers so she can stow her purse?"

Charlie followed Aurora to a side door that she hadn't seen the previous day. Aurora showed her which locker was hers and then handed Charlie a key on a chain.

"Just remember to take that off if you get into any serious play." Aurora pointed to the chain. "You wouldn't want to choke or anything."

"Play?" Charlie repeated.

"The boss doesn't mind if we play on our breaks." Aurora smiled. "That's why we're all here, right?"

Charlie walked back to the foyer as she replied, "Oh, I'm not…"

"Hello, Charlene, you're looking very sexy tonight."

Charlie turned and looked up to see Master Barry taking in her outfit. His eyes were so heated and hungry that her breath hitched in her throat.

"Are you ready, baby?"

"Yes, let's get to work."

Master Barry moved closer and slung an arm around her shoulders. "Stick close to me tonight, honey. The Doms in here can be quite persistent with their demands, but be assured that no one will touch you or make any sexual requests."

"I don't need any help. I've been looking after myself for quite a while now," Charlie said.

"This place is a lot different to what you're used to. The men in here expect to be obeyed by any sub. Even if you're working, not playing, they can be demanding. Do you remember what the club safe word is, Charlene?" Master Barry led her through the crowded room and over to the bar.

"Red."

"Yes, good girl. Just remember to use that word if you find yourself in any trouble. If a Dom asks for your help with anything and you are uncomfortable with what you are being asked to do, use the safe word. Master Turner, myself, or one of the dungeon monitors will come running, but since they all know the rules I don't really expect you to have any problems. But there are always one or two people in a crowd who will push the boundaries of the rules. You and I both know that not everyone is as law abiding as we are."

She gave a nod of her head, letting him know she understood.

Charlie was aware of the curious stares but ignored them. She couldn't believe how busy it was. For some reason she had thought the place wouldn't fill up until much later in the evening.

Master Barry must have seen her confusion. "The club opens at six on Thursday and Friday nights. The members always seem more eager to get an early start as the week wears on."

Over the next couple of hours, Master Barry showed Charlie where everything was kept. He also told her that she should limit the alcohol she served as they didn't want any inebriated patrons. It presented too much of a danger in a BDSM club. Bottled water was to be given away at no charge, though, because it was important to keep hydrated during a scene.

As she worked behind the bar with Master Barry she saw that he was a good man. He was kind to the other subs, be they male or female, and he was fair and compassionate.

Once Charlie was comfortable with what she was doing, she began to take more notice of her surroundings. The cries of pain and pleasure could be heard echoing above the din of chatter, and Doms walked past with their subs. Some of the subs were naked, while others had on minimal clothing such as G-strings and corsets. What surprised her most were the female Dominants, called Dommes. They were decked out in leather and high-heeled boots and often had leashes in their hands as they led their subs. Some crawled on hands and knees, and others walked along with their heads lowered.

She'd never have imagined a woman as a Dominant. Of course she knew that women were equal to men except in the strength department in most circumstances, but she was so far away from wanting to be in control in the bedroom, she knew that scenario wasn't for her.

Charlie paused in her introspection. *Maybe I am submissive after all.* Just as that thought crossed her mind, strong, muscular arms wrapped around her waist. She looked back over her shoulder at Master Barry.

"What just went through your mind, baby?"

Shit! Does he have ESP or something? Has he been watching me the whole time? It seemed nothing got by him or Master Turner.

"Uh, not much," Charlie hedged.

Master Barry spun her around, keeping an arm around her waist so she was pinned up against him. He used his other hand to tilt her face up to meet his gaze.

"I asked you a question, sub. You know the rules. I expect an honest answer. If you lie to me, I will know and then you can expect to be punished."

"Um, I—I was thinking that m—maybe Iamsubmissiveafterall."

"Say that again, Charlene, but this time speak clearly."

"I said"—Charlie enunciated with precise, clear eloquence as well as a bit of attitude—"I was thinking that maybe I am submissive after all."

She held up a finger when a smile began to cross his lips and halted his speech. "But only in the bedroom."

"Finally." Master Turner's voice came from behind her, but when she tried to spin around, Master Barry stopped her.

Charlie looked up into the mirror on the back wall of the bar, her eyes connecting with Master Turner's. He was looking at her with such longing, her body responded to that heat. Her breasts swelled and her nipples engorged with blood to hardened peaks. Her clit began to pulse as it, too, became excited, and cream leaked out onto her panties. Master Turner's eyes traveled down her back and halted at her ass and hips. She shifted on her feet and clenched her thighs together.

"Master Barry, I think it's time you and Charlene took a break. Use the phone and call Master Tank to take over for a while."

Charlie wondered what was going on. Master Turner's expression had changed from hot and hungry to ice cold. *Have I done something wrong? God, I don't like upsetting anyone.*

Master Barry moved his hands to her shoulders and turned her toward the end of the bar. Charlie looked down toward the floor to hide her anxiety and trepidation, but also her anger. What pissed her off the most was that there were at least five Doms sitting at the bar and watching her and the two Masters. If Master Turner was trying to humiliate her for some grievance she didn't even know she had committed, then she was going to give him a piece of her mind.

Taking her time skirting the end of the bar, Charlie finally stopped beside Master Turner.

"You have disobeyed me,, Charlene. You agreed to obey my demands as your Dom, but still you thought you could flaunt my policies. I am going to punish you for not complying with my rules. Do you remember what the club safe word is?"

"Red." At last she gathered the courage to lift her head to meet his gaze. She said indignantly, "I haven't done anything wrong. You shouldn't be punishing me. I haven't even left the bar. For what possible reason can you have to mete out punishment?"

"What was my rule about underwear, Charlene?"

Shit! Oh God, why did I think he wouldn't notice? What is he going to do to me?

She licked her lips nervously and saw him follow that action with his eyes. When she opened her mouth to speak, he once more met her gaze.

"No u–underwear."

"And did you come to my club with panties on?" he asked.

Charlie glanced away, wondering if his question was rhetorical. He knew she was wearing panties. But he seemed to be waiting for her reply, so she whispered, "Yes."

"Take them off, Charlene," Master Turner commanded.

Master Barry came close to her, and she glanced toward the bar to see Master Tank working in their place. His face was expressionless, but he was watching the scene avidly. She glanced toward the other

Doms to see they were just as enthralled with their altercation. She wasn't sure how she felt about having an audience for this.

Charlie took two steps toward the doors, intending to return to the locker/dressing room, but Master Turner's hard voice stopped her. "No. Come back here, Charlene."

She glanced at him and then looked away quickly. He was pointing to the floor right in front of him. Charlie stood where he indicated. "Remove your underwear, sub. Right here."

Charlie gasped and glared at him, but he just held her stare with an implacable look of his own. "I'm waiting. For every second you make me wait, you add to your punishment."

Charlie's pussy clenched and more juices leaked out. The image of being spanked flashed through her mind. *Will he put me over his lap or maybe one of those weird-looking benches?* As she watched him, his eyes changed from cool to heated. Her breathing sped up, as did her heartbeat. With deftness she didn't feel, she slid a hand up beneath her skirt and hooked her thumb into the side of her undies. Tugging them down until they reached mid-thigh, she used her other hand to pull the other side down. Then she tugged them below her knees and finally off over her shoes. She quickly snagged them from the floor and bunched them up into her hand.

"Give them to me," Master Barry demanded.

Charlie passed them over as heat filled her face. She wondered if she was as red as a tomato. Probably. She was about to lower her eyes again, but then she stared as Master Barry brought her panties up close to his nose and sniffed. Her face heated even more, but her body was turned on by the erotic, earthy display.

"Mmm, you smell delicious, sub. Her panties are drenched."

"Good girl." Master Turner threaded his fingers into her hair. He tugged slightly, tilting her head up and back. She didn't have time to think before his mouth was covering hers. He slammed his mouth over hers with a kiss so wild and carnal another gush of her nectar seeped from her pussy to wet her inner thighs.

Charlie couldn't believe how aroused she was at having an audience while Master Turner devoured her mouth. She whimpered as his tongue danced with hers and then he nipped her lower lip. That whimper turned to a gasp when he slid his hand up the front of her skirt and nudged her thighs wider. His caress roved higher and higher until he was just inches away from her pussy.

He lifted his mouth from hers and pinned her with his eyes as he pushed his hand up further and cupped her mound. Charlie sobbed with pleasure as he ground his palm over her labia and clit.

"You like being watched, don't you, Charlene?" Master Turner moved his hand so that his fingers caressed up and down her slit.

She mewled with delight and thrust her pelvis forward, unconsciously begging for more of his touch. "Yes!"

Master Barry walked up behind her and wrapped one of his arms around her middle once more. He pulled her back to his front and held her against him tightly so she couldn't move away.

Master Turner thrust a finger up into her sheath, making her cry out her pleasure. When he began to pump his digit in and out of her cunt, cream leaked from her body continuously, in copious amounts. She groaned as her internal walls tightened. She was on the verge of climax, but that groan turned to a sob of frustration when Master Turner removed his finger from her pussy hole.

"Such a sexy little sub," Master Turner stated and then to her carnal fascination brought his finger up to his mouth and licked it clean. "Hmm, so sweet and musky. I can't wait to eat you out, Charlene."

"If you need any help, Master Turner, just let me know," Master Tank stated from behind the bar.

Charlie whipped her head around and saw the heat in Master Tank's eyes as he perused her from head to toe. Wow, she'd never had one man look at her like that before, let alone three. It did wonderful things for her ego.

"Same goes," another Dom said.

"Me, too," said another. "I would love to get my hands and mouth on that sexy body."

"Sorry, gentlemen, this sub is taken," Master Turner said in a cold, hard voice.

"Pity," called out another Dom. "Is she as soft and sweet as she looks?"

"Even better," Master Turner replied. "Let's take this to the St. Andrew's Cross."

Charlie wasn't sure she wanted to know what that was, but when Master Barry spun her around, bent down, placed his shoulder into her stomach, and then stood back up with her over his shoulder, she knew she was going to find out. Excitement and trepidation warred inside her, but the excitement won out. She wanted this. Wanted to know if the taste of pleasure Master Turner and Master Barry had given her yesterday was a fluke or real.

She had been attracted to them both physically from the first moment she had laid eyes on them, and she felt as though she was beginning to understand Master Barry. Although she was very attracted to Master Turner, too, she still hadn't worked him out. He praised her when she did what he ordered, but when she took her own time or disobeyed him—like wearing underwear—his eyes went ice cold and all expression left his face.

Charlie clung to Master Barry's T-shirt, and then she let go as he slowly lowered her feet to the floor. She hadn't been able to see where he was taking her as her hair had been all over her face, but as she pushed her hair back into some semblance of order, her eyes darted around the room.

She was standing in a room off the great room which had glass along one wall where people could stand and view what was happening inside. There was no door, so anyone could walk in at any time, if they wished. Charlie's breathing escalated, and perspiration began to bead on her palms. She wiped her hands down the side of her skirt and took a step back from Master Barry, only to come to a halt when she bumped into Master Turner.

His breath caressed her ear as he leaned down and spoke to her. "Remove your corset, skirt, and shoes, Charlene."

Charlie gasped when he caressed his hand over her ass and then gently gripped one cheek and then the other.

"But I'll be—"

"Silence!" Master Turner barked out. "Do you want to use your safe word, Charlene? If you use the safe word 'red,' everything stops."

Charlie thought about it, but she was so aroused and drawn to the two men looking at her that she decided to see where this thing she felt was between them could go. If she was honest with herself, the idea of them controlling her pleasure and having their hands and hopefully their mouths on her body fascinated her. There was a need deep down inside that was begging to be released and she had no idea what to do.

"No," she finally answered. "I don't want to use my safe word."

Chapter Four

Barry was so hard it was a wonder his cock hadn't split his zipper open. He had enjoyed working behind the bar with his little sub, teaching her how their system operated and where everything was. Once she had become comfortable with how things worked, she had begun to talk to the other Doms. She didn't flirt with the other men, but she was sassy and courteous, and she also had an almost sweet and innocent quality about her. And she had a body to die for, even if she didn't agree with him. He and Turner were going to have to spend some time with their woman convincing her she was sexy and feminine and that she didn't need to change anything about her.

But she didn't know how to deal with two Doms yet. Charlie was racking up the punishments tonight, and Barry was mentally rubbing his hands together. He couldn't wait to get hold of that sensual little body, and from the way Turner's cock was pushing against his jeans, neither could he.

Barry had watched Charlene avidly during the last few hours, hoping she would make some sort of infraction so he could punish her, but she hadn't messed up once. He was glad when Turner had seen that she had been wearing panties and then ordered her to take them off in front of everyone. She had looked back at his business partner with such belligerence he knew Turner would add the attitude thing to her transgressions.

So far she had two punishments coming, and if she didn't get her ass into gear and get her clothes off, she would add another to the list. She must have seen the determination in Turner's eyes because all of a sudden she began working on the hooks and eyes down the front of the corset and released the closures one at a time. By the time the last hook was out, Barry was holding his breath, just waiting for another glimpse of her beautiful, bountiful breasts. With one hand she held the corset together over her breasts, but after taking a deep breath, she finally let one side go and pulled it from her body.

He nearly groaned out loud when he saw how hard her dusky, rose-colored nipples were. Her breasts looked swollen, and the turgid peaks looked like they were begging to be touched or sucked.

"Very good, little sub," Turner praised. "Now the skirt."

Barry took the corset from her hand and placed it on the chair near the door. He waited with bated breath for her to remove her skirt. This time he and Turner would get to see her pussy. Charlie had balked at removing her panties yesterday when she was being interviewed for the job, and rightly so. He didn't want her doing anything she was too uncomfortable with and was glad that she had the backbone to let him or Turner know when she'd reached her limit. Her fingers fumbled with the zipper, but then she slowly began to lower it. When it was down as far as it would go, she pushed the fabric down over her hips and let the skirt pool on the floor.

"Pick it up and give it to Master Barry and then remove your shoes." Turner stood watching Charlie without any expression at all. She kept giving him furtive glances as if trying to gauge his emotions. Turner had perfected the Dom stance and look, but he had known Turner for so long he knew his friend was just as eager to get his hands on Charlie as he was. She would have been able to see he was eager if she looked down at Turner's crotch, too, but she was more intent on watching his eyes.

When Charlie bent over, he drew in a ragged gasp as her ass muscles flexed and he saw the bare, glistening lips of her pussy. Her thighs were also shiny with her juices. Barry wanted to walk over to her, grip her hips, spread her thighs apart, and bury his face between her legs. His muscles tautened as he gathered his control. Turner was leading this scene, and he was to follow. He would eventually have his time of control, but for now he was taking his prompts from his friend.

"Good girl." Turner moved closer to her and ran his hands down from her upper arms until he wrapped them around her wrists. He began walking backward and led her over to the St. Andrew's Cross, which was a large padded X shape that also had four points where a sub could be restrained by ankles and wrist.

"Step up, honey." Turner held her hands until she was on the small platform and then gently pushed her forward until her front was against the padded cushioning of the cross. He lifted one hand and attached the restraint around her wrist and then nodded to Barry to see to the other one. Barry clasped the restraint around her and then ran his finger under the cuff, making sure that it wasn't too tight. The last thing they wanted to do was cause problems with her circulation or for the leather to cut into her skin. The wide cuffs were lined with lamb's wool for a sub's protection. Together they secured her ankles with her legs spread wide apart.

Barry noticed the slight tremble in her body and quickly stood, bending so his head was close to hers.

"Are you all right, Charlie?"

"Yes."

"Do you want to use your safe word?"

"No," she breathed out.

Barry ran a hand over her hair, down her back, and up again. She shivered, and goose bumps rose up on her skin. "You are such a pretty little sub. We are going to make you feel so good, baby."

Barry stepped away when Turner moved closer to Charlie. He had a leather dildo flogger in his hand. The handle was a black gel tubular dildo, and the leather straps that protruded from the fake cock could be used as a flogger. It was ingenious device as both ends had their use.

Turner ran the leather straps over Charlie's back, letting her feel the toy before he began to wield it. Once Charlie began to relax, he removed the flogger from her back and then flicked his wrist. The slapping noise made Charlie jerk. Though she tugged against the restraints, Barry knew she hadn't felt any pain, because his friend hadn't put much force in the hit. With every flick, Turner added more strength until the flogger began to leave pink marks on their sub's back. He worked his way down until he was flogging her ass. Until that moment, Charlie hadn't made a sound other than her panting breaths, but now she began to moan as the strands of leather connected with her buttocks and she pushed her hips up into the blows.

Barry's cock jerked and pulsed, and his balls ached. He wanted to walk up behind her, release his hard dick from his constricting jeans, and ram his penis into her hot, wet pussy with one shove. He adjusted his aching erection and glanced up to see Turner smiling at him. The urge to touch her was too much, so he moved around the cross until he was standing in front of her. Her face was flushed with desire, her lips were plump and swollen, her eyes closed, and tears were running down her face.

"Wait." Barry held his hand up to stop Turner striking her again. "What's wrong, baby? Is the pain too much?"

"No," she moaned. "It feels so good. God help me but it's not enough."

Using his hands, Barry wiped the moisture from her cheeks and then walked back over to the door, where Turner had dropped his equipment bag as they had entered the room. He grabbed a few tissues and the bottle of water sitting on the floor next to the bag. Barry walked back over to Charlie and held the tissues to her nose.

"Blow," he ordered and was pleased when she obeyed without any hesitation. He then opened the bottle and held it to her lips, letting her quench her thirst. "Okay now?"

"Yes. Thank you."

Barry tilted her face and brushed his lips over hers. She whimpered when he licked the line of her lips, and she opened to give him access. He kissed her hungrily, hoping to quench some of the fire running through his blood, but it only made his desire flame hotter. He kept his eyes open and watched Turner move to stand behind Charlie. With a deft flick of his wrist, he flipped the flogger over and caught the base of the dildo. Barry slowed and stopped the kiss, and after stroking a finger over her cheek, made his way around her to stand next to Turner. He was just in time to see his friend run the tip of the fake cock through her dew-coated slit and then over her distended clit.

Charlie groaned and thrust her hips forward even more. Barry slapped one of her ass cheeks and then admired the pink handprint forming on her pale skin. Just as he smacked the other cheek, Turner began to push the dildo into her vagina. She mewled and moaned as Turner slowly but surely inserted the rubber into her cunt. When he reached bottom, he eased out until the tip of the cock was resting just inside her body. Charlie tilted her hips up again, trying to get Turner to shove the dildo in again, but he held still, waiting for her to stop moving. Barry gave her ass five swats in quick succession, showing his dominance over her, and she immediately lowered her lower body back to the cross.

"Good sub," he said loud enough for her to hear. "You will learn that we control your pleasure, Charlie. Not you. We'll give you what you need but only if you don't try and take that power from us."

"Please." She spoke so softly that she almost whispered, desperation evident in her voice. "I need more."

Turner mustn't have been able to hold his desire back because he relented and rammed the dildo into her to the hilt. Charlie cried out and gasped as he pulled it back out again. With increasing speed, Turner shuttled that fake cock in and out of her pussy until she was keening and her body began to shake. The force of Turner's thrusts looked almost violent, but not once did their woman's cries sound as if she was in pain. She pushed her forehead into the cushioned St. Andrew's Cross as she screamed with pleasure. Barry slid his gaze back to between her legs, where cream was dripping from her pussy as her vagina contracted and released around the rubber phallus. Her anus was pulsing, opening and closing, giving him and Turner a peek of her sexy rosette.

Barry sat down on the platform between her feet, so that he was facing Turner, and then bent down so he could scoot between her legs. He had trouble getting his shoulders in through the X of the cross, but he persisted and half turned until one shoulder was through. He was in the prime position for what he wanted. Her pussy was just below the middle of the X and accessible to him if he leaned forward slightly. Using his thumbs, he separated her labia, and opening his mouth over the top of her slit, he began licking and nibbling on her clit.

Turner withdrew the dildo from her pussy, and Barry slid his tongue through her drenched folds and sucked her delectable cream into his mouth.

"She tastes nice and sweet, doesn't she, Master Barry?"

"Hmm-mmm."

"Listen to the little sounds our sub makes while we are pleasuring her." Master Turner moved closer to him and their woman. "I can't wait to make love to our sub. Would you like that, Charlene?"

"Oh God," she cried when Barry sucked her clit into his mouth, suckling on the sensitive bundle of nerves gently but firmly.

Smack. "I asked you a question, sub. I expect an answer," Turner stated coldly.

"Yes. Please, now."

Smack. "You don't give the orders here, Charlene. We do. I expect you to keep quiet unless I ask you a direct question. Is that understood?"

"Yes."

"Yes what?"

"Yes, Master Turner."

"What a good sub. Very nice, honey. I like it when you speak to me with respect. I think I'll have to reward you, Charlene."

Barry gave one last slurping suck and lick to Charlie's pussy and then slid out from beneath her. Master Turner was already undoing her ankle restraints, so he began to work free the ones around her wrists. Turner wrapped an arm around her waist and pulled her against his body as her legs wobbled and threatened to give out, and then he picked her up and carried her over to the spanking bench.

The spanking bench was waist high and would place a sub in the perfect position for a spanking with their ass tilted up slightly for ease of access, but it was also the optimum position for a Dom to fuck her from behind while she sucked off another.

Turner lowered her to the ground and helped her into position. This time only her legs were to be restrained. Until they ascertained what her hard limits were, they didn't want her to become scared.

"Spread your legs, Charlene."

Charlie complied quickly with Turner's command, and then he restrained one leg with the softly lined ankle cuff while Turner did the other. Barry moved around to the front of the bench and began to remove his clothes. He watched Charlie watch him, pleased to see her eyes glaze over with desire. Her gaze roved over his body, homing in on the waistband of his jeans as he opened them and lowered the zipper. She licked her lips as he slowly eased his pants down over his hips, toeing his shoes off at the same time and kicking them aside. When he stood before her totally naked, he let her look her fill.

Turner moved up behind her, blanketing her body with his naked frame when he knelt on the padded cushion between her legs. "Do you like what you see, Charlene? Does seeing Master Barry's hard cock make you wet? Do you want to have a cock fucking your hot little pussy?"

"Yes!"

Turner yanked on her hair but not enough to hurt her and barked out. "Yes, what?"

"Yes, Master."

"What are you answering yes to, little sub?"

"All of it." Charlie nearly yelled her answer.

"Good girl, Charlene. I like it when my sub is honest."

Barry grabbed the base of his erection and brushed the head of his cock over Charlie's lips. She opened her mouth and flicked her tongue across the top, no doubt tasting the pre-cum leaking from his tip. He grasped her hair and pushed inside her moist cavern. At the same time, Turner, having donned a condom, began to penetrate her pussy. The moan she hummed around his cock reverberated up and down his shaft, heightening his pleasure. As he withdrew to the tip, she hollowed her cheeks and suctioned firmly, creating a wet, pleasurable friction on his hard cock. Then she swirled her tongue around the head of his dick and laved the underside.

She reached out to take his cock into her hand but stopped when Turner slapped her ass. "Put your hands back on the side of the bench, sub," he gasped between breaths, "or we'll have to restrain you."

Charlie placed her hands back on the sides of the padded cushion and gripped it so hard her knuckles turned white. Barry held back his smile then shifted his gaze back to her mouth to watch his cock sliding in and out between her lips. The sound of flesh slapping flesh prompted him to look over to Turner, and he saw sweat beaded on his friend's face as he fucked Charlie from behind at a rapid pace. If he hadn't seen it before, he would have thought Turner was being tortured by the look on his face rather than being pleasured.

"Do you like having my cock in your mouth and Turner's in your pussy, Charlie?"

"Mmm," she agreed on a hum.

"Fuck! Your mouth feels so good, baby. I'm going to move faster. If you can't handle what I do or don't like it, just lift your right hand. Okay?"

"Mmm."

Barry increased the pace of his thrusting while holding her head still with a hand in her hair. She began to hum continually, and the noises she made grew louder, unconsciously or maybe consciously letting them know she was getting close to climax. Turner gripped one of her hips firmly and then he moved the other hand down between her legs. He didn't have to see what his friend was doing to know that he was thrumming her clit.

Her humming turned to gasping cries, and just in time, too. Barry's balls were trying to crawl up into his body as the tingling warmth at the base of his spine spread around to his crotch. It wouldn't do for him to come before their woman.

Just as he thought he was going to go over first, Turner did something to make her scream. The sound was muffled as Barry shoved his cock into the back of her throat and he watched her right hand in case he was giving her more than she could handle. But her hand remained still, and she swallowed around the tip of his cock. That was all it took. Fire enveloped his balls and traveled up his shaft, expanding his size slightly, and then he was shooting from the tip. He roared her name as ropes of cum erupted from his dick. His climax was so strong his muscles quivered and his legs shook.

Turner's yell joined his, and he froze behind Charlie, emptying his jism into the condom. When Barry's cock stopped jerking and he felt as if his balls had turned inside out as they'd emptied, he slowly withdrew from her mouth as Turner eased from her pussy.

He rushed to Charlie and uncuffed her. Turner got rid of the condom and went to dress, but since Barry had a head start, he was fully clothed first. He lifted her into his arms and held her tight. She was shaking and snuggled her face into his chest. When Turner had finished pulling his clothes on, they helped her put her skirt and corset back on and then Barry lifted her again.

He carried her from the room while Turner stayed back to clean the equipment. Barry settled onto one of the semi-secluded sofas and cuddled Charlie until her shaking slowed and then finally stopped.

Master Turner sat down next to them and lifted Charlie's feet to his lap, caressing up and down her shins and lower thighs, soothing her down from her climactic high.

After about fifteen minutes, Charlie shifted on his lap, and he knew she was back with them once more. It always amazed him how deeply flogging, spanking, and then making love affected a sub's equilibrium, but he figured it was an erotic high, the same as a Dom experienced from being in control of a sub's pleasure. Adrenaline and endorphins mixed with pleasure and pain was a powerful thing.

Barry wanted to keep her in his arms. Charlie felt so right, her weight comforting against his body. He'd never felt like this before, and from the way Turner was watching her and touching her, he hadn't either. She felt like home, and he intended to do everything he could to keep her in his bed and hopefully end up in her heart. He knew it was quick to have such feelings about a woman he had only met the previous day, but he was thirty-three years old and had enough experience to know when something felt right.

Charlene was a mix of innocence and sexual wantonness, wrapped up in a soft, warm, beautiful package. He couldn't wait until she really let go. Though he and Turner had tapped into her passionate side tonight, he knew there was more.

What gave him pause and worried him the most was the way the unattached Doms had been watching her so avidly. And they still were. He could feel their eyes on them, on her, from their positions at the bar and other seating areas around the room. Some Doms only played with subs once and moved on to another as they either weren't ready to settle down as yet or hadn't quite found what they were looking for in the subs they enacted scenes with.

He only hoped that he and Turner had gotten to Charlie on an emotional level and that she wanted to see more of them and play with them on a regular basis. But he wasn't about to push in case she balked.

Barry would speak to Turner later and suggest they give her a collar. If she wore Turner's and his collar, then the other Doms would know that she was claimed and off-limits. He knew it was too early to ask that of her, but he wanted it so bad, to know that she was his and Turner's without having to worry about the other Doms coming on to her.

He hoped when his friend and colleague asked her to wear their collar, she accepted. He would feel more secure in regards to their little sub if she were under their protection.

Chapter Five

How long Charlie sat on Master Barry's lap while Master Turner caressed her legs, she had no idea. She couldn't believe how content and cherished she felt from being flogged and then made love to by Master Turner and Master Barry. After she had screamed her climax it had felt as if she had been floating on a cloud, and she hadn't wanted to come back to earth. She'd never experienced such a powerful, bone-jarring orgasm in her life, though she hoped she would again.

But it wasn't just the physical side of things that drew her to these two men. The way they had wiped her tears and given her water had been acts of concern, as was the way they held her now. It seemed almost loving.

She was drawn to them more than she had ever been drawn to anyone before, and the thought of not seeing them or being with them caused her pain. She never would have believed she would become aroused by being flogged and spanked, much less having a dildo shoved up her pussy. Charlie knew she was a bit of a prude. Her sister Charity had told her often enough and she had come to believe her. But now she wasn't sure what to think or believe. Everything she'd ever thought about herself had just been blown out of the water.

Why do I feel this way?

But what flummoxed her the most was how much she had enjoyed being restrained and letting them make love with her after knowing them for such a short time. She'd never done that before. Her own behavior and acquiescence astounded her, and she wasn't sure how to handle this side of her personality. Charlie was shocked over how turned on she had been by the many eyes which had been upon her as Masters Barry and Turner had taken control away from her and how much she enjoyed being the center of attention when normally she liked to blend into the background. And then there was the fact that she was at work and had had an orgasm. Who got to do that? Certainly no one she'd ever encountered. She was so far out of her comfort zone she didn't know what to do, to think, or how to feel.

She pushed herself into an upright position and sighed with reluctance as first Master Turner and then Master Barry released her, and she finally rose to her feet.

"Are you all right, little sub?" Master Turner's voice was more emotional than she'd ever heard it, and he smiled at her with a sparkle in his eye.

"Yes, thank you."

"Don't thank us, baby. We should be thanking you." Master Barry paused and drew in a breath. "Are you ready to get back to work, or do you need more time to gather yourself?"

"I'm fine."

"Good, then let's get to it."

She began to follow Master Barry back to the bar, but Master Turner placed a hand on her wrist. "I'll see you before you leave this evening, Charlene. Make sure you wait for me before you go home."

"Yes, Sir."

"Such a good little sub." Master Turner caressed her inner wrist with his thumb and then released her.

Charlie worked steadily through the night, chatting with the friendly Doms and steering clear of the ones who weren't so friendly. But she couldn't get her mind off the scene with Masters Turner and Barry. Her pussy felt swollen and every time her mind drifted back, cream leaked onto her thighs. She had never thought that being ordered around and then giving up all control would be such a turn-on. She just hoped that the two Masters were as pleased with her as she was with them. If their shouts of completion were anything to go by, they were. Charlie couldn't wait for them to make love with her again. Her heart skipped a beat and her breath hitched in her throat at the thought of submitting to them once more.

Charlie shook herself out of her reverie, accidentally making eye contact with a man who had been staring at her all night. It was making her uncomfortable. She didn't want to say anything to Master Barry and cause a stir since the man was doing nothing wrong, but if she encountered him again after tonight, she might just give the man a mouthful. With less than an hour to go before her shift finished, Master Tank came and took over from Master Barry.

"I'll be back before you leave, Charlie. Make sure you don't go anywhere if I'm delayed. I'll be walking you out to your car."

"Yes, Sir."

She watched Master Barry walking across the room, weaving through the throng of people until he got to the door with the number pad, and then he was gone. Charlie sighed. He was such a big, handsome man and she had liked watching the muscles in his ass move and the ones in his shoulders and back ripple as he walked.

"Oh, you have it bad, don't you, little one?"

Charlie turned to Master Tank and stared without replying. He gave her a smile and a wink as he filled a drink order. She worked up and down the bar, handing over drinks and collecting money, but she avoided the man still sitting at the end watching her. Knowing that she was going to have to eventually ask him if he wanted another drink, she took a deep breath and then headed down there.

"What would you like?"

"Oh, darlin', you shouldn't ask a Dom a question like that." His voice was deep and gravelly like his throat or voice box had been injured. She wasn't turned on by the sound or attracted to his handsome countenance.

Charlie just stared at him and waited for him to answer her question, but he just sat there looking at her from the top of her head down to her waist where the bar hid the lower half of her body. On his way back up, his eyes snagged on her breasts and stayed there.

Drawing in a deep, annoyed breath, she decided she had had enough of his rudeness.

"Hey, buddy, my eyes are up here. If you don't want anything to drink, just say so and I can get back to serving others who do."

That seemed to snap him out of whatever trance held him, and his angry gaze met hers. His jaw clamped down hard and his body tensed, and he stood up from his stool. Then Charlie was being hauled over the bar by the front of her corset. He moved really fast and she hadn't had time to stop him. He held the top of her corset in his large fist, his knuckles and fingers digging into her breasts. The glass that had been on the bar in front of him fell to the carpeted floor with a dull thud as he pulled her across. Charlie yelled as her hips and thighs scraped over the edge of the wooden bar, and then she was on the other side, falling to her knees, which burned as they skidded on the carpet at his feet. She cried out with pain when he fisted her hair with such force that some of it was pulled free from her scalp.

Just as Charlie yelled, "Red," her hair was released and she scrambled from her hands and knees to her feet. Master Tank looked downright furious. He had the cruel Dom by the scruff of his shirt, his other large hand around the asshole's wrists. Judging by the tendons and muscles standing out on Master Tank's forearm, he was exerting a lot of strength.

Some of the other Doms who had been sitting at the bar talking came over to help Master Tank as the other man tried to fight free of his hold. The twin Doms Luke and Matt Plant took over from Master Tank and dragged the bastard toward the exit.

Master Tank gently took hold of her arms and looked her over. She was already close to tears, and the concern she could see in his eyes was the catalyst that made her lose control. Tears pricked the back of her eyelids. "Are you all right, sugar?"

Charlie didn't think she could answer without a wobble in her voice, so she just nodded. Master Tank must have seen she was barely keeping it together and drew her into his body, wrapping his arms around her.

"Shh, sugar, it's over now. Did he hurt you?"

Charlie pushed her face into his chest as the tears began to flow. She didn't want anyone to see how weak she was. Although her hips and thighs felt bruised and her scalp was sore from where her hair had been ripped out, she was fine. When her body began to shake with reaction, Master Tank held her tight against him with one arm around her waist and caressed her head and hair with the other.

Then she was being transferred to another pair of arms. Her body stiffened for a moment but then she relaxed when she inhaled the familiar lemony scent of Master Barry. He cuddled her close and then picked her up into his arms with ease, as if she weighed no more than a feather. He held her firmly.

"What the hell happened?"

Master Tank explained the incident to Master Barry, who cursed loud and viciously. Soon Master Turner was up against her, too, and she was sandwiched between the two muscular Doms, Master Turner's warmth and pine scent comforting her as the shakes finally waned and stopped.

Master Turner stepped back and gently nudged her face away from Master Barry's chest. His eyes roamed over her face, and his expression turned hard. She tried to pull away and hide again, but he wouldn't let her.

"Carry her through to our private rooms." Master Turner spun on his heel and led the way.

Charlie saw other subs and Doms looking at her curiously, but she didn't meet their eyes. She snuggled into Master Barry's embrace and wrapped an arm around his neck.

Master Barry walked down a long corridor with doors leading off them. He stopped at the end while Master Turner unlocked another door and entered. The doorway opened up to a very large, comfortable living room, and she realized that she was in their private rooms.

Master Barry lowered her feet to the floor and then reached for the hooks on her corset, releasing them from the metal eyes. She reached up and covered his hands. "What are you doing?"

"Checking you over for injuries."

"I'm fine."

"You will let Master Barry remove your clothes, little sub," Master Turner commanded and stepped up behind her to lower the zipper on her skirt.

Charlie looked over her shoulder and saw the implacability in Master Turner's eyes. She removed her hands and lowered her arms to her sides. She bit back a sigh of longing as the two Doms stripped her. They were taking such good care of her, which she wanted to continue. She wanted to be with them all the time. Although she had only known them for just over twenty-four hours, she felt like she had known them her whole life. They seemed to fit her somehow, but she wasn't about to say anything in case she came across as needy. Hopefully she would have a lot more time to get to know them.

But then she thought about the trouble she had caused with that bastard Dom by giving him lip. They might not want her working for them anymore. His reaction had been way over the top as far as she was concerned, but she was new to the lifestyle and didn't know all the ins and outs of BDSM protocols. For all she knew she was the instigator of that little scene at the bar because she had stood up for herself. But maybe she wasn't supposed to have said anything at all.

"What are you thinking about, baby?" Master Barry's voice drew her from her introspection.

"Um, just the Dom who pulled me over the bar." Master Barry studied her as if he knew she was omitting a lot of detail, but she wasn't about to give him insight into how her brain and emotions worked. At least not yet. It was way too early.

"Damn, you have the beginnings of bruises on your hips and thighs, and your knees have carpet burn." Master Turner walked around her, looking her over. "Where else did he hurt you, Charlene?"

"He ripped some of my hair out when he grabbed me."

"If Chad Hilton hadn't already been kicked out and banned from the club, I would cheerfully go find him and beat the shit out of him," Master Barry snarled angrily.

Charlie lowered her gaze and bit her lip. *Are they angry with me? Was I supposed to take the lewd stares and comments from the other Dom? Are they going to fire me now?*

"I'm sorry," she whispered.

"Why are you sorry, Charlene?"

Charlie lifted her head and met Master Turner's eyes. "I'm sorry for the trouble I caused. I understand if you don't want me working here anymore."

"Damn it, Charlie!" Master Barry exploded. He gripped her shoulders and gently turned her to face him, cupping her cheek so she was looking him in the eye. "You have nothing to be sorry for, little one. That asshole has been pushing his luck for months. Chad Hilton has had more complaints against him than the entire state senate. He treats subs with contempt, like they are there to be used for his own personal harem."

"Master Barry is right, Charlene. I have been looking for an excuse to ban that asshole for weeks. It was unfortunate you're the one who had to suffer to get him ejected." Master Turner had come around to stand next to Master Barry as he spoke. When she opened her mouth, he placed a finger over her lips and continued. "I'm not sorry I had to kick that fucker out. What I am sorry about is that he hurt you. We should never have left you alone. That was unforgiveable as far as I am concerned."

"It wasn't your fault. You had Master Tank helping me out and watching over me." Charlie reached out and took one each of their hands. "You couldn't have known what he would do."

"No, we couldn't, but you are under our protection. One of us should have been nearby."

"Hindsight is a wonderful thing. If we all could see into the future and stop ourselves from making mistakes or knew what each and every day held for us, then we would be very boring and jaded."

"She's right, you know," Master Barry said and clasped her hand a little tighter. "If we knew what life held for us, then there would be no excitement in our lives. None of us would learn from our errors or gain wisdom as we grew."

"And here I thought I knew what life was all about. When did you get to be so wise, baby?"

Charlie shrugged, not sure how to answer that. She didn't think she was super intelligent, but she knew she wasn't dumb either.

"I think you should have a bath." Master Turner picked her up and carried her toward the hallway.

Charlie wrapped her arm around his neck for balance. "You're going to hurt yourself. I'm too heavy to carry. Put me down."

Master Turner ignored her until he had carried her into a large, opulent bathroom. She stared at the massive spa bath and then turned to look at the large glassed-in shower. There were lots of showerheads sprouting from the wall, and the cubicle was big enough for at least four people. He slowly lowered until her ass connected with the granite counter in between two sinks with gold fixtures.

Master Barry had followed them into the room, and as Master Turner turned the faucets on and checked the water temperate, he pulled his T-shirt over his head. She salivated as his muscled shoulders and pectorals and his ripped abs came into view. Unconsciously licking her lips, she followed his hand down to the fastening on his jeans.

"What are you doing?"

Master Turner spun around and looked at her. "Are you allowed to question a Dom, little sub?"

"No, Sir."

"Good girl." Master Turner then removed his T-shirt.

Charlie wanted to jump off the counter, go over to both men, and touch them. She wanted to run her hands all over them. She wanted to touch their hard bodies and warm skin, and she wanted to lick them all over.

"You'd better stop looking at us like that, Charlene. You are in no condition for any loving."

Charlie perused Master Barry's naked body. Moisture dripped from her pussy, and her internal muscles clenched. They were both such handsome and sexy men, Charlie was having a hard time concentrating with all that buff, bronze skin in front of her.

She drew in a gasp when Master Barry scooped her up into his arms and stepped into the tub. He had removed the rest of his clothes while she had been studying his gorgeous body, and as he sat down with her on his lap, Master Turner stepped into the tub and sat at their side.

"What…"

"Shh, little sub, just sit back and relax while we take care of you." Master Turner picked up a sponge and squirted some bath gel onto it. He picked up her arm and began to wash her, while Master Barry held her still with an arm around her waist.

The more Master Turner attended to her, the more her libido stood up and took notice. Charlie's breasts and nipples engorged, the peaks turning into hard tips. Her pussy clenched and released cream, begging to be filled. When Master Turner ran the sponge over her lower belly and then down to her sex, Charlie pushed her hips up involuntarily. The action had been so instinctive it was as if her body had taken over.

"Barry, sit on the edge and take her with you."

Master Barry lifted her with ease so that they both sat on the edge of the tub. Her legs were over his, and when he splayed his thighs, hers were spread wide open. Then Master Turner was washing between her legs with the soap-slick sponge. He was gentle but thorough. Starting at the top of her slit, he lightly rubbed her clit and then down through her delicate folds.

"Hmm, you smell so sweet," Master Turner said in a deeper voice than usual. "I can't wait to make love with you again."

"Ooh," Charlie groaned as he washed around her pussy hole and then pushed until a tiny bit of the sponge edged just inside her.

"You like that, don't you, baby? I have to have a taste of that sweet cream."

The two men brought her back into the water and rinsed her off. Soon she was sitting on a towel, back on the edge of the tub with both men kneeling before her. Master Turner kept his gaze pinned on hers as he lowered his head. With the first swipe of his tongue through her moist labia, he growled against her flesh, sending vibrations running through her pussy and causing her clit to throb with need.

Master Barry reached up and took one of her nipples between his finger and thumb and pinched firmly while he got up onto his knees. He sucked the other nipple into his warm, wet mouth. Charlie sobbed and arched her chest and then her hips up for more of their touch.

Then Master Turner laved the tip of his tongue over her clit and rimmed her pussy hole. Charlie was so overwhelmed with pleasure she didn't know whether to push them away or beg for more.

When Master Barry released her nipple with a pop, he then leaned up and covered her mouth with his own. He ate at her lips, sucking on her tongue and lips rapaciously. She cried out with pleasure as Master Turner thrust a finger up inside her pussy. Her muscles clamped down around his digit as he sucked her clit into his mouth. Charlie whimpered with frustration when he removed his finger from her body, but when he pushed two back into her sex, that whimper turned into a mewl of delight.

"Yes, that's it, little sub. Give me your cream and let go."

He pumped his fingers in and out of her pussy, passing the pads of his fingers over that sweet spot inside that she'd heard every woman had but had never discovered for herself. Master Barry weaned his lips from hers and kissed his way down her neck and chest. He flicked his tongue over the tip of her breast in time with Master Turner's tongue rasping over her sensitive little pearl.

The dual sensations were enough to send her rocketing to the stratosphere. Charlie threw her head back and screamed. Her whole body shook with cataclysmic pleasure as wave upon wave of ecstasy swept over her. The two men didn't stop touching her until the last quiver faded away, leaving her spent and so satiated that her eyelids were too heavy to keep open.

She let them slide closed and sighed when strong, muscular arms wrapped around her waist and she was lifted from the tub. Charlie floated in the zone between sleep and wakefulness until she was laid down on cool sheets and let her conscious mind drift away.

Chapter Six

Turner snapped his eyes open and wondered what had pulled him from a deep sleep. Since he had served in the military and then security he had learned to be on alert in an instant. A slight breeze washed over his face, and he reached out to the middle of the mattress where Charlie should have been. The space was empty but still warm. His hand connected with Barry's and he quickly pulled back again.

How did the little vixen get out of from between Barry and me without me feeling her move?

With a sigh Turner flung the covers aside and swung his legs over the side of the mattress and then sat up. Muted light was coming from under the door, and he wondered where Charlie was. He pulled his jeans on sans underwear and went in search of her.

The living room light was on, but Charlie's clothes were gone from where he and Barry had left them on the floor. Checking the door to his rooms, he saw the lock had been disengaged. Charlene Seward had cut and run.

With another sigh, he headed toward the kitchen and the coffeepot. Just as he poured the hot, dark brew into a mug, Barry entered.

"She's gone?"

"Yes. I didn't wake up until it was too late. Fuck. What are we going to do?" Turner slammed his hand down on the counter.

"There's not much we can do at the moment. What time is it?" Barry asked, picking up his mug and walking over to the table where he sat down. Turner followed him.

"It's just after three."

"Well, we'll just have to make sure we spend as much time as we can with her. Maybe we scared her off by acting out a scene with her and the incident with Chad was just another catalyst."

"Why would she be scared?" Turner scrubbed a hand over his face. "He's an asshole and deserves everything he gets."

"You and I know that, but it was Charlie's first night working for us. She's submissive down to the bone and has a poor self-image. To have to confront Chad must have been hard for her, and then to find out he was banned would make her feel culpable."

"Yes, you're right. Damn it, normally I understand exactly how a sub's mind works. Why is it that we are reversing our roles here?"

Barry leaned back in his chair. "Because we both know that she is the right woman for us."

"I don't follow."

"Charlie's exposed our own fears as much as she's shown hers. I'm a little afraid of pushing her too quickly emotionally and you...you are worried that if she sees what an arrogant, controlling bastard you are that she will turn tail and run." He paused. "I mean that in the nicest way possible."

"She turned tail and ran anyway," Turner said with a frown.

"Charlie's not running from us. She's running from herself."

Turner mulled over that statement and realized that Barry was right. Charlene Seward was scared of what they made her feel. He and Barry were going to have to set up a scene and try to get into her mind. If they could work out what she was running from and why she was so scared of what she was feeling, then maybe they would be able to move ahead and have a relationship with her.

"I think you're right. Who do we have coming in tomorrow night as dungeon monitors?"

"Let me think." Barry pondered. "Tank as usual. And I think Wayne and his brother Warrick as well as Kenny and Nate. Why?"

"I want to keep at least one of them watching our sub when we play with her. You know as much as I do that when we're in the moment we can miss things. Plus one of the others can help Tank work the bar while we are otherwise occupied."

"Hmm, what do you have in mind?"

"I think we should do a scene on the stage near the dance floor." Turner rubbed his chin. He was getting an idea of what she needed. He and Barry spent over an hour talking and planning. Once done they headed back to their own beds to try to get a few more hours' sleep.

As Turner lay on his back staring at nothing in particular, he tried to figure out why Charlie was afraid of her feelings. He wanted to know everything about her, including her family and previous boyfriends. There was usually a reason for a woman to run. She had obviously been hurt before and didn't want to commit on an emotional level, but he and Barry weren't about to let her get away with that. He realized how deeply he already felt for Charlie and he knew he and Barry could have something really special with her, if she'd open up with them. Turner had learned to watch subs very closely, but with Charlie it was different. When he watched her he picked up every little nuance of emotion, expression, and body language she portrayed. And because he was so attracted to her, felt more intimately tethered to her, he was able to read her more clearly than anyone else he knew besides his longtime buddy. They wanted everything from her and they were just the men to take it.

* * * *

Charlie once again found herself looking in the mirror, perusing her plump body and the way the new outfit she'd bought that afternoon fit over her round hips and full breasts.

God, why do I bother? All I ever see is cellulite.

She turned away and slid her feet into the black three-inch heels and hoped her feet wouldn't ache too much. Though she was used to wearing heels all the time, she still felt the effects by the end of the evening.

Tonight she was wearing a dark purple corset and midthigh-length black leather skirt. The clothes were so different from what she usually wore, but the change made her feel almost sexy. Maybe when she looked in the mirror she didn't actually see reality. Maybe her mother and sister had been wrong about how she looked. She closed her eyes a moment and took a deep breath. When she opened them again she tried to look at herself from a stranger's point of view. For a moment she almost believed that she was pretty and only slightly overweight, but then the same image she usually saw stared back at her. She felt really uncomfortable and vulnerable wearing something so out of the norm to what she usually dressed in. Tugging at the top of the corset didn't make any difference. The tops of her breasts still bulged up and out. And pulling on the leather skirt didn't make it any longer either. As far as she was concerned she had way too much flesh on display. No, make that way too much flesh on her body, period. With a sigh she reminded herself that she couldn't change the way she looked or the extra twenty pounds she'd carried since she could remember. She snagged her keys and purse and headed for the door.

As she drove she thought about the previous night with Master Turner and Master Barry.

Why did I let them touch me? I am so weak when it comes to those two men? God, what the hell am I going to do? I can't have a relationship with two men! What do they see in me?

When she had woken in the early hours of the night she hadn't known what she was supposed to do. She wasn't experienced enough to know what men expected from her after spending the night with them. Or part of the night, anyway. Would they have been horrified to wake up and find her still in their bed? She didn't want to come across as too clingy or needy, so she had very carefully crawled to the bottom of the bed and snuck into the living room, dressed, and left.

How the hell am I going to face them after what happened last night? She didn't know what they expected from her and she had no clue as to what they wanted with her. *Oh well, Charlie. What else is new? You've never been good with men, so why would this be any different?* She gave herself a mental shake and pushed her thoughts aside.

Charlie looked around and realized she was sitting in her car in the parking lot of Club of Dominance with the engine idling.

Shit, girl, you could have had an accident zoning out like that. Thank God I seem to be able to drive on automatic pilot.

Charlie turned off the ignition, got out of the car, and locked the door. She wasn't eager to see Master Turner and Master Barry, so she slowly made her way to the front entrance. Master Tank and Aurora were in the entrance, greeting clients and signing them in. Master Turner insisted that all staff and patrons sign in each time they entered the club, apparently for safety reasons. It had something to do with making sure only members were allowed in as well as giving a head count in case of an emergency.

"Charlie." Aurora smiled and bounced up and down. The young woman was so full of energy she was never still. "You look hot, girl." The smile faded from Aurora's face. "That asshole Chad was here asking about you, but Master Tank kicked him out."

Charlie felt fear skitter up her spine and shuddered. Master Tank must have seen her trepidation.

"Don't worry about him, Charlie. He'd have to get past me to get to you and I can't see that happening anytime soon." Master Tank gave her an encouraging smile and she lowered her eyes to the floor.

"Thanks," she replied and gave a weak smile. Her eyes slid over to Master Tank, who was perusing her with a hungry gaze. She looked away quickly, feeling a little uncomfortable with the masculine attention. Charlie walked toward the locker room to stow her purse, and when she came back out, Master Barry was leaning against the counter and staring at her.

"Charlene, please come here."

The inner doors to the club opened as she took a step toward Master Barry. She stumbled when she met the cold stare of Master Turner. *Fuck, is he angry with me? What did I do?*

"I gave you an order, sub." Master Barry's deep voice drew her attention. He was pointing to a spot on the floor right in front of him.

Charlie lowered her eyes and took the necessary steps until she stood where he indicated, but instead of looking up and meeting his eyes, she kept hers lowered. She stiffened when she felt a frisson of awareness at the nape of her neck and then the heat of another body. She knew Master Turner had to be standing close behind her. A shiver of apprehension raced up her spine. She felt totally exposed with her hair up in a ponytail, the back of her neck on view to the club owner. Charlie had no idea why she felt that way, she just did. When fingers lightly caressed the side of her neck, she shuddered with awareness but still didn't look up.

"Look at me, Charlene," Master Barry ordered. Although she tried to ignore the directive, Charlie found herself complying.

Damn it! When will I find some backbone with these two men?

Charlie jerked when something slithered around her neck. She reached up to touch but her wrists were caught in Master Barry's hands and he pulled her arms back down to her sides.

"What are—"

"Silence!" Master Turner's cold voice snapped out from behind her. "You do not have permission to talk, sub."

Charlie lowered her eyes quickly, hoping that Master Barry hadn't seen how truly pissed off she was getting. She should have realized that hope was futile. These two Doms seemed to notice everything she did.

"Didn't I tell you to look at me, Charlene?" Master Barry said in a deep, growly voice.

She was feeling a little rebellious, so she kept her eyes on the floor. "Yes."

Smack.

Charlie wanted to rub her stinging butt where Master Turner had swatted her but refrained since she didn't want to make the two men any angrier than they already seemed to be.

"Ow. What was…" She half turned as she began to speak.

Master Turner lifted his hands near her throat once more and then withdrew them. Charlie felt the leather necklace drop onto her skin. Then his hands were on her hips. He spun her around and placed a hand on her cheek, tilting her head up to meet his icy green eyes.

"I've had enough of your hiding and rebellion, little sub. You read the rules of this club, and we've been patient with you, but this is going to stop right now."

"But I—"

"Enough!" Master Turner growled. He looked over at Master Tank. "Do you have any cuffs?"

Charlie glanced at Master Tank and then Aurora. Master Tank's face was completely blank, but Aurora was looking at her with sympathy. Without a word, Master Tank handed over wide leather cuffs lined with fur. Before she could protest, Master Turner had her wrists restrained and linked together behind her back. Charlie tugged and pulled but gave up when she found no weakness.

What happened next left her breathless and filled with anxiety. Master Turner bent down, placed a shoulder at stomach level, and lifted her. She was slung over his shoulder like a sack of potatoes and he was walking toward the internal club doors.

Even though she was nervous, wondering what he and Master Barry were going to do to her, her body was at war with her mind. Charlie's breasts swelled so much they began to ache, and her nipples formed into hard little peaks just begging for attention. Cream leaked from her pussy onto her thighs, her sheath clamping and releasing as if begging to be filled. And her clit was throbbing so much she was scared she was going to orgasm right then and there.

Charlie struggled, but when another hard slap landed on her ass, she gave up. She could see other Doms and club members watching them curiously. Master Turner carried her toward the raised dais off to the side of the empty dance floor and then he went up the three steps. He carefully lowered her to her feet and made sure she was steady before releasing her. People around the club moved closer or stopped in their tracks to watch. Heat suffused her cheeks and she hoped she wasn't as red as she felt. She saw Master Kenny and his brother Nate, as well as Masters Wayne and Warrick watching her closely, so she closed her eyes to shut them out. She had learned the names of a few Doms the previous night as she served them drinks. Although they were all handsome, brawny men, they didn't hold a candle to her Masters.

Fuck, Charlie. They aren't yours. Get that thought out of your head right now.

Master Barry stepped up onto the stage and held her cheeks between his very large, masculine hands. "You were told that all Doms in this club should be addressed as Master or Sir, were you not?"

Charlie looked off to the side and nodded.

"Do not ever look away from me again, Charlie. When Master Turner or I give you an order, we expect to be obeyed. Do you understand?"

"Yes, *Sir.*" Charlie put as much sarcasm as she could into the "Sir."

Something brushed over her head and then covered her eyes, and all of a sudden Charlie was sightless.

"Hey!"

Smack.

"If you say one more word, Charlene, I am going to gag you," Master Turner whispered against her ear. "You have racked up so many punishments that your ass is going to be too sore to sit down. Hook her up."

Charlie clenched her teeth but stayed silent. She didn't want to give him or Master Barry another reason to punish her. *Or do I?* Her pussy leaked more juices onto her thighs. Her body seemed to have other ideas about punishment.

The cuffs holding her wrists together behind her back were released, and then her arms were raised above her head. She heard a clank and a click, and the hands holding her arms up withdrew. Charlie pulled, gasping when she realized that her arms had been hooked up to the chains dangling from the ceiling. She tugged again, knowing she wouldn't be able to escape but still compelled to try. Another set of hands landed around each of her ankles and then her legs were spread. Restraints were wrapped around her legs, and when she tried to close them, she couldn't. There was something between her limbs keeping them open.

She felt more exposed than ever before, being up on the stage and unable to move or escape, but underlying the nervousness coursing through her body was desire. She was becoming so aroused that the trepidation she was feeling was being pushed back. Heat coursed through her at the knowledge that Master Barry and Master Turner could do whatever they wanted with her.

Charlie felt the numerous pairs of eyes on her and shifted slightly only to have another slap land on her cloth-covered ass. Thank God she still had her clothes on. No sooner had that thought crossed her mind than she flinched when she felt hands at the top of her breasts unhooking the first clasp of her new corset.

"What is your safe word, little sub?" asked Master Turner.

"Red," Charlie panted.

Smack.

Shit. That slap had hurt. Her left ass cheek, where the hard hand had landed, was hot and tingly, and that heat traveled to her pussy, causing more moisture to leak onto her thighs.

"What was that, sub?"

"Red, Sir."

"Very nice," Master Turner praised and ran a soothing hand over her ass. She could tell it was him behind her because of his unique masculine pine scent and his deep voice. Inhaling deeply, Charlie took that scent into her nostrils and involuntarily sighed.

The hands at her bodice belonged to Master Barry and he went back to unhooking her corset. His skin was warm, and as he brushed against her flesh, shivers traversed her spine. She tried to contain her body's reaction but she wasn't sure if she had managed it. The deep chuckle from in front of her told her she hadn't.

"You can use the safe word anytime you want to stop this, Charlie."

She gave Master Barry a nod to let him know she understood and then cried out as another slap landed on her other ass cheek.

"Yes, Master," she squeaked quickly.

"Good girl."

The corset fell away, exposing her body to anyone who cared to look. Cool air wafted over her skin, making her already-hard nipples form into tighter buds. Then her skirt was being removed, and she pulled against the restraints, wanting to prevent her rounded stomach from being uncovered, but of course she couldn't.

Charlie didn't want to use her safe word and wondered why she wasn't screaming it out at the top of her lungs. It took her a few moments to realize that even though she didn't like her body, deep down she liked being watched. It heightened her awareness and desire knowing she was standing up on a dais where anyone could see her. Maybe she was a closet exhibitionist. She didn't want anyone else touching her other than Master Barry and Master Turner, though. Was she a pervert? The thought of someone else laying their hands on her body was repugnant.

"You are such a beautiful woman, Charlie. So damn sexy, I get hard every time you come near me."

Charlie let out an inelegant snort which earned her another slap on her ass. This time there was no cloth barrier between her flesh and the smack. The tingling warmth she'd felt every time that hand landed on her butt was so much more intense, and more of her cream dribbled down her inner thighs.

Warm, moist breath caressed her ear, and then Master Turner's hands were running up and down her back and sides. "Why did you take off last night, Charlene?"

Charlie didn't want to answer that question, so she closed her mouth, pulling her lips in against her teeth.

"Our little sub is going to be stubborn," Master Barry said.

"Yes, so I see," Master Turner replied and then he whispered in her ear again. "You will tell us everything we want to know, little sub. Don't think we are going to let you get away with not answering."

Charlie heard rustling off to her right and then a low buzzing sound. Something soft rubbed over her body, starting on her belly and then slowly working its way up to her chest. She was so achy with arousal she arched her body into the touch.

"Yes, you like being touched and on display, don't you, Charlene?"

She didn't know if she was supposed to reply, so she stayed mute.

"Do you think we can't see your arousal?" Master Barry asked. "Your sweet, sexy pussy is glistening with your juices and so are your thighs. Your nipples are hard little nubs just begging for our touch."

Swish.

Charlie cried out with surprise and the heat and tingles swept over her belly. There were numerous impact points but when the thing hit her again, she realized that she was being flogged with hide straps. Was Master Turner whipping her with a flogger?

The buzzing she'd heard came closer and then her whole body jerked as that vibration lightly touched her clit.

Oh God. They have a vibrator.

Charlie was panting and straining forward for a firmer touch to her pussy. Just a few more swirls of that vibrator would be enough to send her over the edge into climax. Licking her dry lips, she thrust her hips out, eager for more.

Master Turner kept flogging her, making sure to spread his hits out over her body and ass. The dual sensation of pleasure and pain was so good. Charlie didn't want it to ever end.

Just when she thought she was going to go over, they stopped. She cried out with frustration and pulled on the restraints.

"You don't get to come until you answer our questions, little sub." Master Turner tugged lightly on her ponytail. "Why did you leave last night?"

"I didn't think you'd want me to stay," Charlie said after carefully thinking about her response.

"We would never have brought you into our home if we hadn't wanted you there, Charlie. Try again," Master Barry said.

Shit. Aren't I allowed to keep my deepest secrets and thoughts private?

Charlie yelped when the flogger connected with the back of her thighs and sobbed out with pleasure as the vibrator was slowly inserted into her pussy. The two men kept her desire so high that all she needed was one slight touch to her clit and she would explode. But they were Doms and weren't about to let her have what she wanted until they had what they wanted.

How can I be so in tune with two men I have only just met? Why do I feel like I have known them my whole life? Why did it rip my heart out to leave last night? Why do they feel so right? Why am I so drawn to them?

Why? Why? Why?

Chapter Seven

"Why? Why? Why?"

Charlie was sobbing and chanting, and fear clutched at Turner's heart. *Did we push her too far and too fast?*

Turner dropped the flogger onto the floor and began unclipping the cuffs from the chain. When they came free he slowly lowered her arms and massaged them to get the blood flowing back into her limbs. As he worked on her upper body, Barry removed the vibrator from her pussy and removed the spreader bar.

When she was free, Turner swept her up into his arms and hugged her tight while Barry removed the blindfold. And then he stepped down from the stage and over to one of the sitting areas.

Charlie was still saying the word "why" over and over again as her tears flowed nonstop. She buried her face against his neck when he sat down on the sofa and cradled her tightly against him. Barry wrapped her in one of the blankets piled on the glass coffee table and then sat next to them, lifting her legs over his lap and stroking her shins with his hands.

Charlie's tears seemed to be never ending, and even though he wanted to know why she was crying and why she had so much pain inside her, he didn't say anything. He held her close and waited patiently. He looked at Barry and saw that his friend looked just as tortured as he was as they witnessed her grief. But that patience eventually paid off because finally her tears slowed and stopped.

"I'm sorry." Charlie's voice was muffled since her mouth was against the skin of his neck. "I don't know what came over me."

Turner leaned back and nudged her face up. "Don't you dare lie to me, Charlene! I won't have it!"

"Darlin', why were you crying?" Barry reached out and clasped one of her hands.

She looked from Barry, up to him, and then back to Barry again.

"You aren't leaving until you've told us what's going on in that pretty little head of yours, so I suggest you start coming clean, little sub."

Charlie took a deep breath and slowly released it. She placed a hand on his chest and pushed herself into a more upright position. Turner tightened the arm he had around her waist, silently letting her know she wouldn't be getting away from him.

"I didn't like the way you made me feel."

"What?" Barry's eyes iced over. "You didn't like the way we took care of you and then helped you relax by making you come?"

"No. Yes. Shit."

"Take your time, baby. Get your head together and then explain." Turner kissed her temple and hid the smile as she expelled a sigh full of longing. In a way he was glad she had broken down. Now maybe they could get to the crux of why she held so much of herself back.

"I liked the way you made me feel," she said almost defiantly.

Now that she was over her upset, she was getting back to her normal self.

"I have never let a man I've known only twenty-four hours touch me. I don't date because the men I have gone out with are always making comments about my body. Telling me I could do to lose a few pounds or eat less and so forth. My mom and sister never said one nice thing about me the whole time I was growing up. Every time I was interested in a boy, my sister always ended up going out with him." Her breath hitched audibly. He rubbed his hand up and down her side, offering comfort and support.

"My sister is a very famous model. I'm sure you've heard of Charity Seward." Charlie thrust her chin up defiantly. "My mom kept telling me I should be more like my sister. 'Charity is so beautiful and slim, why can't you be more like her? You eat too much, Charlie. You need to exercise more.' Well, in the end, I got so fed up trying to please my mom and sister, I gave up and decided they weren't worth it."

"Good for you, darlin'." Barry kissed the back of her hand.

"Okay, so because of your mother and sister, you think you're fat. Is that right?" Turner asked.

"Yes." Charlie's response was so quiet he almost didn't hear it.

"We'll deal with that in a moment," Turner said. "Why did you think we didn't want you to stay in our home?"

"I'm not sure what the protocol is. Okay? God, I haven't had a date in over three years. And I wouldn't consider the last asshole I went out with once a 'date.' I don't go out at all. I spend my free time reading or watching television."

Agitated, Charlie shifted on his lap, but he held her firmly.

"I liked that you and Master Barry took care of me. I like the way you both touch and kiss me. No, I didn't just like it, I love it. But I was scared I was coming across too needy, too clingy. What man wants a woman clinging to him like a vine?"

"You aren't a clinging vine, baby." Turner sighed. "In fact, we can't get enough of you. Not that there is anything wrong with your independence, but we want more. Don't you know we care for you, Charlie?" Turner's voice was deep and husky with emotion and he mentally cursed his use of her nickname, but then he thought that she needed to know how he felt, so he was glad he let her hear the emotions in his voice.

"How can you? You don't even know me."

"Now that's where you are wrong, darlin'." Barry shifted in his seat. "You are a stunningly beautiful woman. You have a heart of gold and have so much love to give. If only you'd let us in. We want your love, Charlie. You are a natural-born sub and we want to explore that with you. I'm already half in love with you, little one. Please don't shut us out."

"Barry's right, Charlene. You've already worked your way under my skin and into my heart. Please, just give us a chance to let us show you how good it could be between the three of us."

"That's another thing. How am I supposed to date two men? I am going to come across looking like a slut."

Turner gripped her chin and held her gaze. "Don't you ever call yourself that again! You are so far from being promiscuous it's almost laughable. We won't let anyone say anything disparaging against you, Charlene. We will take care of you, of that you can be certain."

"I—I don't know." She hesitated, her gaze sliding away once more.

"Yes, you do."

"You should let me go. I'm supposed to be working."

"No. I already have Tank and Thomas working the bar tonight. We are going to stay with you until you understand what it is we want with you." Turner set her on her feet and held her hips until she was steady. She clutched the blanket closed around her body and took a couple of steps away from him.

Turner was on his feet in an instant. He wrapped an arm around her middle and pulled her back against his front. "Stop. Whatever you're thinking, don't. I want to prove something to you. Come with me."

He looked over at Barry and gave him a nod, knowing his friend would understand what he wanted. Turner removed his arm from her waist and took hold of her hand, leading her back toward the stage. It was slow going as the club had been filling up with a constant stream of members since he had put a stop to their scene. The dance floor was packed with Doms and subs dancing, kissing, and playing. He glanced down at Charlie when he heard her gasp and followed the direction of her gaze.

There was a threesome practically making love on the dance floor. Two Doms sandwiched their sub between them, one of the men was fucking her with his fingers, while the other played with her breasts and kissed along her neck. Charlie's breathing escalated and he saw the pulse at the base of her neck jump and then speed up.

Oh yes. Their little sub was a voyeur as well as an exhibitionist. She was perfect for them.

When Turner started up the steps of the stage, Charlie balked and tugged on his hand. He turned and bent down to whisper in her ear so she could hear him over the loud music. "We aren't going to play, baby. I just want to show you how wrong you are about a few things. Do you trust me, Charlene?"

While he waited for her answer, he noted how tight his muscles were. She had already showed him that she trusted him and Barry a couple of times. First by stripping down to her panties in the interview and then by letting them play with her last night, but that was before her crying jag. When she gave him a nod he stared deeply into her eyes and let her see how much she meant to him and cupped her cheek. Moisture gathered in her eyes and she quickly blinked it away. Turner led her up the dais, Barry close at their heels. He caught Tank's eye and made a slashing movement and waited for him to stop the state-of-the-art sound system. When the music died there were a few moans but once the members, Doms and subs alike, saw him with Barry and Charlie up on stage the noise quieted down.

Turner raised his voice so all the Doms in the back could hear him. "I want all the Doms up front. The rest of you can go about your business." He waved his fingers in a shooing motion and then waited as the twenty or so Doms in the room crowded around the stage. "Thank you. I want an honest opinion on something. You are to look only. No touching, but please don't hesitate when I ask what you think."

He turned toward Charlie and wrapped an arm around her waist. When he glanced at Barry, he saw his friend's smile and the knowing look in his eyes. Barry gave him a nod and a thumbs-up, letting him know he approved of what he was about to do. And then Barry moved up behind her, placing his hands on her shoulders. Charlie was looking a little flushed as she clutched the blanket to her. Keeping her body covered with a tight grip, Turner gave Barry a last look and then prepared to grab hold of their sub because he knew she was going to balk. Taking a deep breath, he nodded at Barry.

Barry whipped the blanket away and threw it toward the back of the stage where Charlie couldn't reach it. As her cover was pulled away, she tried to hide her pussy and breasts, but Turner grasped her wrists in his hands and lifted them above her head. He passed her to Barry to restrain. The position pushed her breasts up and out, drawing attention to her delectably full breasts and hard nipples.

"Shit," Charlie muttered and then lifted her head to glare at him. "What are—"

"Did I give you permission to speak, little sub?"

Charlie's lips drew into a tight line, but she continued to glare and scowl at him. But underneath that intrepid look was the glaze of heat and arousal. She may not even realize it, but their little woman liked being on display. Turner glanced down to her pussy and held in a smile of satisfaction when he saw her wet labia and glistening thighs. Stepping back to her side, he placed a hand on her shoulder as he turned to face the Doms crowding around the stage.

"I would like to introduce you all to our newest club employee and our sub, Charlene Seward. She is new to the lifestyle and will no doubt have a few infractions as she learns the rules, but if she does, all of you will come to either me or Master Barry. This little sub's discipline is ours to give. No one but Master Barry or I will touch her. Is that understood?"

The Doms watching them nodded and gave affirmative answers to his question.

"Good. Now Master Barry and I would like to hear what you think of Charlene's body." Since Turner still had his hand on Charlie, he felt a tremor run through her and her muscles stiffen. Glancing over, he noted she was trying to mask her expression but without much success. He could see her anxiety, and her body language was practically screaming how uncomfortable she was.

"If you hadn't already claimed her, I would have." Master Tank was looking at Charlie as if she were his last meal. "She has the face of an angel and a body like Marilyn Monroe."

"That she does, Master Tank, thank you."

Charlie was staring at Master Tank as if he had two heads. Her mouth was hanging open, and then her eyes quickly slid away. Turner knew it was going to take more praise from the other Doms before she started believing how truly gorgeous she was.

Master Gabe stepped closer. "Look at me, sub."

Charlie, being the natural submissive that she was, couldn't help but comply, and Turner hid his smile behind a stoic façade.

"You have the body of a goddess, little one. If you were mine I would tie you up and spend hours licking over every inch of your lovely, soft skin. Is she as soft as she looks?"

"As soft as silk," Turner replied.

"Lucky bastards," Master Gabe muttered.

"Look at those beautiful full breasts and ripe berries on top," Master Nick stated in a husky voice. "They would look so pretty adorned with nipple clamps. And that hourglass figure is so fucking sexy it's a wonder every man here isn't on their knees paying homage to your woman."

Turner smiled as the compliments came thick and fast, one after the other. All the time the Doms spoke, he watched Charlie avidly. The incredulousness left her eyes, and she stood up a little straighter. The juices leaking out onto her thighs were a testament to how the Doms' words and her exhibitionism were affecting her.

"Thank you, gentlemen, I believe I have achieved my goal. Please feel free to return to whatever it is you were doing."

The Doms began to leave, giving their sub lingering looks of desire and then turning away with sighs of resignation. Turner moved around in front of Charlie and looked her in the eyes. "You are the sexiest, most beautiful woman I have ever seen. If I hear you making derogatory comments about your body again, I will either tie you down and spank you or put you over my knee. Is that understood?"

"Yes, Sir."

"Good. Now I believe since you were such a good little sub and behaved well, you should be rewarded. Don't you think so, Master Barry?"

"Oh absolutely." Barry slowly lowered Charlie's arms, massaging her shoulders and upper arms.

Turner nodded to Barry, and his friend slid his hands down her arms and gently but firmly clasped her wrists behind her back. Bending down, Turner took her mouth with a hungry rapaciousness that even surprised him. Slanting his mouth this way and that, he tasted every inch of the interior of her mouth with his tongue.

Charlie whimpered, and he felt her body soften when she leaned back against Barry. He slowed the kiss until he was sipping at her lips, and then he began to lick and nibble his way down her neck and chest. When he reached one of her breasts, he sucked the turgid peak into his mouth and suckled firmly, and then he brought his free hand up and caressed through her slick folds.

Turner groaned at the copious amount of moisture he found, and he had to clamp down hard to control his own desires. He wanted to kneel down at her feet, shove his head between her legs, and lick and suck her to completion. But he was a Dom, and control was everything.

He crushed her nipple against roof of his mouth with his tongue, and his cock jerked against the zipper of his pants when she cried out. Releasing the peak with a pop, he shifted to her other breast, giving it the attention it craved and not wanting to neglect her needs. His fingers were soaked with her cream and he wanted to feel her heat.

Turner slowly pushed a finger up inside her and then withdrew it to the tip. He imagined the feeling of thrusting into her pussy until he was balls-deep. The mental image made him feel needy, but first he wanted to taste her.

He licked his way down her torso to her softly curved belly and stopped to rim his tongue around her navel. The sounds coming from her mouth told him she enjoyed everything he was doing to her and that she was lost in her pleasure. Charlie was totally oblivious to the fact that they were still up on the stage for all to see.

Turner added another finger to her pussy and began to pump them in and out of her wet hole. She was so fucking tight he wanted in her body now, but still he held back. Bending even lower, he slid his tongue through her pussy lips and then laved over her clit. She bucked her hips forward, showing him how much she wanted his mouth and hands on her. He wanted her to come in his mouth, craved more of her cream, so he gently drew her clit between his lips and sucked, all the while thrusting his fingers in and out of her sheath.

Charlie's internal walls trembled and rippled around his digits, and she screamed her orgasm. Her hips bucked, and she continued crying out as he ate her pussy and fucked her with his fingers. He slurped and drank down her cum until the last shudder of pleasure waned and she slumped in Barry's hold. Turner kissed her inner thighs as he slowly withdrew his fingers, and then he kissed her mound before rising to his feet.

His little sub was a sex goddess. Her eyes were closed, and she looked totally boneless in Barry's arms. Her lips were swollen and her cheeks were tinged a deep pink hue from her climax.

Barry swept her off her feet and transferred her into his arms. Turner held her close while his partner retrieved the blanket, and between them they wrapped it around her body. Charlie sighed and snuggled against him, the touch of her nose to the skin of his neck eliciting feelings he'd never had before. He looked down at Charlie with awe, hesitating midstride. He'd known from the beginning that she was right for them, her being a natural sub and having such a sweet personality, but he'd never expected his heart to become engaged.

Turner cared for her, and so did Barry. They'd both told her so, but he'd never thought to feel so full of emotion. The thought of her not being with him by his side and in his bed made pain rip through his chest. *God, I'm in love with her.* He'd heard of love at first sight, but being the arrogant, cynical Dominant that he was, he had been a skeptic. It seemed the writers, poets, and songwriters were right after all.

He glanced over his shoulder as he walked toward the keypad door and saw the same emotions in Barry's eyes. Taking a deep breath, he waited while his partner keyed in the code and held the door open for him and he walked through.

Although he wanted to tie her up and spank her ass until it was a pretty pink, he needed to feel her hands and mouth on him. It looked like his dominant tendencies were going to take a backseat for a while. He needed to make love with their woman.

Chapter Eight

What is happening to me? Am I truly into all this kink?

She had just climaxed on a stage in the middle of the great room where all and sundry could watch. She wasn't an extrovert, yet she had relished being the center of attention. Being watched by all those Doms had only cranked up her libido to a higher level. Feeling cherished as she snuggled into Master Turner was already mind blowing, but remembering what she had done made her heart pump hard all over again.

She'd read a lot of romance books over the years and even erotic romance novels from ménages to BDSM, and although she'd enjoyed them all, Charlie hadn't ever thought she was a sexual deviant. But it looked like she was wrong, because she had been so turned on when Master Turner had kissed, touched, and licked her in a room full of people. The thought of him and Master Barry fucking her while others watched sent her arousal firing up from its satiated state.

"What just went through your mind, little sub?" Master Barry asked as Master Turner lowered her to the bed.

God, she'd been so caught up in her thoughts she hadn't realized they were in the Doms' suite of rooms, let alone the bedroom.

"Um, I was wondering what was happening to me," she whispered and lowered her eyes to the floor. She was sitting on the side of the bed with her legs hanging over the edge. Charlie wanted to feel in control and moved so her feet were touching the floor.

"Look at me, Charlie," Master Barry demanded. "You are submitting to us, baby. Don't overthink what's happening. Just think about how it makes you feel to give up control to us."

"It's freeing, isn't it, baby?" Master Turner said from behind her. "Imagine how good you are going to feel once you let everything go. We won't ever hurt you, Charlene, but we will push your boundaries to make you feel good. Now, look at Barry liked he asked, little sub."

Once again Charlie found herself complying. She sighed with frustration at her obedience but looked at Master Barry. God, his eyes were beautiful. She felt as if she were drowning in the deep blue pools. His expression was blank, and Charlie was beginning to think she'd done something wrong. Then he smiled at her, and her breath caught in her throat. He was such a handsome man and was looking at her as if she were the only woman left on the planet. But underlying the sexual hunger was so much emotion that tears pricked the back of her eyes.

She let her attention slide to the side, only to connect with Master Turner's gaze as he moved around in front of her. She gulped, trying to control her reaction to what she saw in his eyes.

"You are the most beautiful woman I have ever met, Charlie." Master Turner knelt down so his face was almost level with hers. "Will you stay here tonight? We want to spend the rest of the evening making love with you."

Charlie knew she should protest. She was supposed to be here to work. In the last two nights she hadn't finished a shift out yet. But she also wanted to feel their hands and mouths on her body. She wanted to be able to touch them and taste them and show them how much they meant to her. The last thing she wanted to do was drive home after the evening was over and climb into her lonely, cold bed. The need to be wrapped up in their arms was a yearning she couldn't ignore.

"I—I…"

Oh God. I'm in love with them.

"What are you thinking about, Charlie?" Barry questioned.

Charlie didn't want to answer that question. She didn't want to come across as needy, and if she told the two Doms how she felt and they didn't reciprocate her feelings, she was going to end up with a broken heart. The need to push them away became paramount so they wouldn't know how much she cared.

"You two employed me to do a job. I think I should get to work. I can't spend the hours here playing. I need to earn money to pay my way in life."

"We will still pay you for the hours you are here, Charlene."

Charlie flinched with indignation and then rose to her feet. She avoided looking at either Dom and looked around for her clothes, since she had seen Master Barry with them in his hands as Master Turner had carried her toward the internal door.

"Damn it, Charlie," Master Turner said in a heated voice, slipping again and using her nickname. She hesitated as she remembered him also using her nickname when saying she was the most beautiful woman he had ever met. It was unusual for him to slip up, because he was usually so controlled, and the heat in his deep voice contrasted the almost cold quality it normally held. If he really cared for her he wouldn't have said what he just did. "That didn't come out right."

"You're telling me," Charlie muttered and then walked out of the room. Before Master Turner had spoken she'd cherished every moment she had spent with them. After what he'd just said she wanted to crawl in a shower and scrub away the remembrance of their touch. She felt used and almost…dirty. *Is that how they think of me?*

Sighing with relief, she spied her skirt and corset on the sofa and hurried over to them. She had her skirt on and was trying to do up the corset when it was ripped from her.

Charlie turned and raised her arm to cover her breasts as she faced the two Doms. Master Turner had a look of contrition on his face but she also saw implacability, and his stance showed pure determination. Well, this time she wasn't going to obey either of them. If they were going to say hurtful things, she wasn't going to just go along with them, whatever they wanted from her. Pain throbbed in her chest, and although she wanted to rub over her heart, she wasn't about to let them see how much she was hurting.

"I didn't mean that I was paying for your services, little sub." Master Turner scrubbed a hand over his face and then ran it through his hair. "All I meant was that you wouldn't lose any pay for following our orders. We are the ones who have taken you away from your duties. You have to understand I've never done that before."

Master Barry took the corset from Master Turner and stepped forward. She was appreciative when he wrapped it around her and began to hook it up. Charlie didn't like feeling so vulnerable and naked after what the club owner had said. When Barry had fastened the last clasp, she stepped back.

"I'm sorry, Charlene. I never meant to hurt you or for my words to come out as derogatory. I just wanted you to know you wouldn't be penalized in a monetary way for our actions."

She saw the sincerity in his eyes and knew he meant what he'd said. He'd fucked up and now he was trying to make amends. Charlie had wanted to spend the night with them both, making love with them, but now she needed some time to get her head together. Every person she'd met in her life ended up hurting her, including her family. She didn't need it from these two arrogant assholes, too.

"I accept your apology." She thrust her chin out and placed her hands on her hips. "But I think it would be best if I got back to work."

Charlie hesitated as her hand landed on the doorknob. She looked back over her shoulder to the two men. "I think we should keep things between us platonic. This would never have worked."

She wanted to prove that she meant it. They could read between her words so well that she feared they'd know how her heart cried out against walking away. She looked down, trying to think of a way to show she meant it, and noticed the leather collar they'd given her.

She'd seen other subs wearing collars in the club. From what she understood, it meant the sub was off-limits to other Doms. She didn't want any other Doms to touch her, but she didn't care for Turner and Barry to do so either.

Releasing the doorknob, she undid the collar from around her neck and dropped it on the floor.

She left the suite of rooms and headed back down the hall. Taking a deep breath, she opened the entrance door to the club and hurried across to the bar. Master Tank and Master Thomas were working there and gave her quizzical looks when she began filling orders. She ignored them.

* * * *

"Damn it, Turner. You just made a huge mistake," Barry snarled as he faced his friend.

"You think I don't know that?" Turner spun away and then back again. "Fuck! How could I have been so stupid? I've never been so out of control in my life."

"We have to get her back. Shit." Barry began to pace. "I love that woman so damn much there is no way I can live without her."

"I know that. I feel the same. God, I've pushed her away and that wasn't what I intended. I hurt her so damn much and just when we were beginning to make her feel good about herself. She's been wearing our fucking collar, for Christ's sake. If she thinks she can just walk away from what we have, she has another thing coming."

"So what are we going to do to get her back?" Barry stopped his pacing and pinned Turner with his eyes.

"God, I don't fucking know. I have no clue when it comes to Charlene. She has me tied up so much inside I feel like my gut is one large ball of string."

"We can't let her leave tonight. Not with how upset she is."

Turner sighed and strode toward the door, glancing back toward him as he tugged on the door handle. "We are going to go and sit at that bar and try and get back into her good graces. If she is still standoffish by the time her shift ends, then she stays here with us."

"You can't make her stay if she doesn't want to, Turner. God, you can be such an arrogant asshole."

Turner flipped him off and then his shoulders slumped as he sighed again. "I know I can't, but if I tell her she is going to stay she will comply. Haven't you noticed she obeys our every command?"

"Of course I have. What sort of Dom would I be if I didn't take note of how she reacts to us? That beautiful woman is so close to letting go, and we are the only ones who are going to be near her when it happens. Charlie has only given us a glimpse of her submissive nature. You and I both know there is so much more to her. She is a sexy, passionate woman. I can't wait until she is living here with us."

"Me, too." Turner pulled the door open and walked down the hall. Barry followed him, hoping that Charlie would be willing to accept Turner's apology and forgive and forget. As far as he was concerned, once a tiff was over it was finished. But what was most important right now was getting her to talk to them first.

* * * *

Charlie was facing away from the bar as she read off the recipe card of the exotic drink she was making when the back of her neck prickled in warning. Glancing up into the mirror on the wall, she saw Master Turner and Master Barry approaching. She mentally cursed as her cheeks heated and she saw that her skin was flushed. Charlie hated that every emotion showed up on her pale skin. Quickly lowering her gaze back to what she was doing, she tried to concentrate and prayed they would go away. As she poured the orange juice into the glass her eyes snagged on the mirror once more. The two Doms were staring at her, and she knew she wasn't going to get away with avoiding them.

When she spun around, her eyes on the glass in her hand, she walked to the other end of the mahogany bar and placed the drink in front of the Dom who had ordered it. "Thank you, little sub."

Charlie scowled but quickly looked away when she realized it was a dangerous thing to do to such a dominant man. When he chuckled, her tense muscles released and she began taking orders from the patrons close by. She was hoping to stay down this end of the bar, away from Masters Turner and Barry so she wouldn't have to speak to them.

Master Tank met her in the middle and nudged her gently with his hip to get her attention. Charlie didn't want advice, but the look on Master Tank's face said he was going to butt in whether she wanted his words of wisdom or not.

"I don't know what has you so sad, Charlie, but you need to talk to them about it. They aren't going to let you keep on avoiding them."

Charlie felt tears prick the back of her eyes, Master Turner's words still ringing in her ears. She sighed and blinked a few times to dispel the moisture in her eyes. There was nothing she could do about the ache in her chest or the beating her pride had taken not so long ago, but she wasn't about to let herself be pushed around by anyone else. They all thought she was submissive. Though she wanted to refute that claim, she wasn't about to waste her breath. But she wasn't going to let herself be pushed around any longer. Spinning around to face Master Tank and placing her hands on her hips, she glared up at the big brute of a man.

"I don't need you or anyone else telling me what to do. So back the fuck off, *now*."

Master Tank's concerned gaze flashed from warm to cold in an instant. His muscles rippled and hardened as he crossed his arms over his chest and thrust his hips forward in an aggressive move.

Uh-oh, what have I done? Charlie lowered her eyes and took a quick step back. She was about to take another when Master Tank's hard voice stopped her.

"You will not back away from me, Charlie, but you will apologize."

"I'm sorry," she whispered.

"What was that, sub? I didn't hear you."

Charlie raised her head and looked at Master Tank. His eyes were gleaming with amusement but his face was still expressionless. "I'm sorry, Master Tank."

"Much better." He ruffled her hair like she was a little kid. "Now I think you need to go and talk to your two Doms."

Charlie stepped back and shook her head as she lowered her eyes once more. She didn't want to talk to Master Turner or Master Barry. She was still hurting inside. "I have work to do."

Charlie worked for the next hour, avoiding the area of the bar where her two Masters sat drinking water and watching her. She tried to keep her gaze from them, but it was an impossible task. When her eyes met Master Barry's, they seemed to snag as he held her gaze. No matter how hard she tried to look away, she couldn't. Then movement to his side drew her attention, and she met Master Turner's green eyes. He rose to his feet, never taking his eyes from her, and skirted around the end of the bar. Charlie took a step back with every forward step he took. The muscles in his arms and shoulders rippled as he stalked toward her.

God, he is so damn hot. Why do I have to be in love with him and Master Barry?

Charlie gasped as she felt herself drowning in his green pools. *What is he going to do?* She thought, placed a hand over her pounding heart, drew in a ragged breath, and finally managed to drag her eyes away from his. She let out a squeak when her back connected with the counter to the side of the bar. She was trapped and had nowhere to go. Master Turner stopped in front of her. He was so close she could feel the heat emanating off of his body, but she kept her eyes lowered.

"Look at me, Charlene." His voice was hard and brooked no argument or rebellion.

Charlie found herself once more looking into the depths of his eyes. When he raised a hand up and cupped her cheek, she wanted to pull away from his touch, but she couldn't get her body to obey the command of her brain.

"I'm so sorry, little one," Master Turner said with such sincerity it brought tears to her eyes. "I never meant to hurt you, Charlene. I didn't mean what I said the way it sounded. Will you please forgive me?"

The tears she had been trying to contain spilled over and rolled down her cheeks. Charlie believed that Master Turner was contrite and hadn't meant to demean her in any way, but she wanted so much more from him and Master Barry. She loved them. *God, I want to spend the rest of my life with them. But that will never happen. I know they said they care for me but that isn't enough. I want more.*

She finally conceded with a nod of her head and tried to step back.

Master Turner moved quickly, lowering his hand from her face and grasping her around the wrist. "Will you please come and talk with us?"

Charlie finally found her voice, even if it did come out a little raspy. "Okay."

"Good girl." Master Turner removed his hand from her wrist and wrapped his arm around her shoulder. "Tank, if you need help, call one of the other Doms to give you a hand. Charlene won't be available for the rest of the night."

Charlie glanced at Master Tank, and he gave her a smile and a wink. "No problem."

Just as Charlie was about to pass him, Master Tank bent down to whisper in her ear. "Give them a chance, little one. They care for you."

Master Turner led her out from behind the bar and headed across the great room toward the door leading to their private quarters. The tears she had shed had stopped, thank God, but her face felt a little tight and sticky. She wanted to go to the bathroom and clean up, but the way Master Turner was holding her firmly, she didn't think she'd get the chance to do that for a while.

He led her over to the sofa and sat down beside her. Master Barry closed the door to their rooms and then sat on her other side.

"From now on I want you to call us Turner or Barry unless we are playing, all right? We want more than just a Dom/sub relationship with you, Charlie. You are equal to us everywhere but in a scene or the bedroom. When we aren't playing or making love, you can call us by name without any title."

Charlie nodded but couldn't bring herself to speak. She was afraid that if she opened her mouth right now that she would blurt out all of her feelings, and she wasn't about to make a fool of herself and suffer rejection. She didn't think she could stand another upset tonight. *The ache in my chest hasn't let up even after Master Turner... Shit, how am I going to call them by their first names when I am used to adding a title first?*

"What are you thinking about, Charlie?" Master Barry drew her from her introspection, and she looked up to find him studying her avidly.

She just shrugged. "It doesn't matter."

"Oh, that's where you are wrong, little sub. Everything about you matters."

Master Turner took hold of her chin gently and turned her face until she was looking at him. "What is it going to take for me to gain back your trust?"

"I don't know," Charlie whispered. It wasn't that she didn't trust them, because she did. She would never have let them touch her body and make love with her if she didn't. But she was scared she would end up with a broken heart, and that was something she wasn't sure she could deal with. Already Master Turner had hurt her, and even though the ache over her heart was dissipating, she didn't know if she wanted to open herself up for more of the same.

"What if Turner lets you tie him up?" Master Barry asked, drawing her gaze.

Charlie's heart stuttered and then beat heavily inside her chest. Her breath hitched in her throat as her imagination took over. She could just imagine how she could explore Master Turner's body to her heart's content. To have the ability to touch, caress, and make love with him when he couldn't command or touch her in return had her panting heavily.

"Oh, I think our woman likes that idea, don't you, baby?" Turner stated in a voice tinged with facetiousness.

Chapter Nine

Barry watched the pulse at the base of Charlie's neck flutter and then beat rapidly. Her breathing increased, and she unconsciously licked her lips as she stared at him. It looked like he was right. Charlie seemed enthralled with the thought of tying Turner up and having her way with him. He wondered if she would feel the same about him. *No time like the present to find out.*

"What if we let you tie us both up, Charlie? Would you like to be able to touch and taste us whenever and however you wanted?"

Barry held in his smile when she made a small squeaking sound and nodded her head. She was staring at him as if he was the last piece of chocolate on earth, and he knew how much women loved their chocolate.

He wasn't about to wait any longer. If having him and Turner tied up and at her mercy would gain back her trust and respect, then so be it. Barry just hoped after she'd had her way with them that they could talk her into staying with them *permanently*. She'd worked her way under his skin and into his heart. It didn't matter to him that he hadn't known her for very long. He was old enough and experienced enough to know when he met the right woman. And Charlene Seward was definitely that woman. He loved her and wasn't about to let her go. Barry was going to do everything within his power to win her over.

He looked over her head at Turner and knew he was in the same boat as Barry was and was thinking exactly the same thing. Turner gave him a slight nod and then looked back to Charlie as Barry rose to his feet.

"Come on into the bedroom, darlin'. I'll help you restrain Turner and then you can tie me up." Barry offered her a hand and waited to see if she would take it. All three of them knew he was asking her to give them another chance, and he and Turner were hoping like hell that she would accept that they weren't infallible since they were only human.

When she moved and placed her hand in his, he released the breath he hadn't been aware he was holding in, and the tension in his shoulders dissipated. When he glanced at Turner, he saw a flash of relief run across his friend's face.

"Thank you, sugar." Barry helped her to her feet and led her toward Turner's room since it was closest. "You won't regret it. We will do everything in our power to see we never hurt you again."

Turner entered the room as Barry led her to the bed and seated her on the edge. They stood side by side and looked down at her.

"You are to give the orders tonight, baby," Turner said in a huskier voice than usual. "We will obey your every command."

Charlie nibbled on her lower lip uncertainly as she eyed them both up and down. Her cheeks turned a pink hue, and Barry wanted to ask her what just went through her head, but he waited patiently instead.

"I want you to both remove your clothes, please?"

Charlie's order came out more like a question, and as he reached up to pull his T-shirt off over his head, her cheeks turned an even deeper pink. But when he looked into her eyes after he threw his shirt aside he could see the barely contained excitement in them.

She shifted on the bed and squeezed her legs together. *Oh yes, our little sub is very aroused.* He bet if he moved closer and inhaled he would be able to smell her musky arousal.

Turner was naked before him, and Charlie couldn't seem to take her eyes of his friend's hard dick. When it pulsed and jerked, she licked her lips. Barry stepped forward and placed a hand on her shoulder. She jumped as he startled her and then looked up into his eyes.

"What do you want us to do now, darlin'?"

"Um." Charlie tilted her head as she pondered.

She obviously couldn't make up her mind because she didn't say anything else.

He decided to help her out. "Do you want me to tie Turner up?"

"Yes!" Charlie answered enthusiastically and then said in a softer tone, "Please."

Turner got onto the bed and lay down in the middle. He unselfconsciously spread his arms and legs so Barry could restrain him. There were cast iron rings on all four bedposts, and the wrist and ankle cuffs were always kept in the bedside drawer. Barry retrieved them and shackled his friend to the bed.

"Okay, sugar, he's all yours. What would you like me to do?"

"Uh, hmm, maybe you could just sit off to the side for a bit."

"Okay, sugar. Just let me know if you need anything."

Barry sat down on the chaise lounge off to the side of the bed near the wall and waited to see what Charlie would do. He was in the perfect position to watch all the action as well as her face once she started. Barry wondered if their little sub would be able to go through with what she wanted. It hadn't taken him long to work out that she was shy and introverted as well as inexperienced in regards to sex. But underneath all that was a tiger waiting to emerge. He would bet his last dollar that Charlene Seward was hot and wild in bed once she really let go. Of course he and Turner had had a taste of her passion, but Barry knew there was so much more that they hadn't tapped into.

He had gotten to know her over the last couple of nights when he had worked alongside her, and he loved what he had learned about her. She had a wonderful sense of humor when she wasn't feeling threatened and tense, and she wasn't scared to talk with the members while she worked. Barry had seen how a few of the other Doms had eyed her speculatively. Without her knowing about what he was doing, he had stared the other men down and staked a claim. Turner had made claim, too, with the collar she had worn around her neck.

He and Turner hadn't taken the time to explain about the collar and made a mental note to talk about it later tonight.

She climbed onto the bed and then sat back on her heels and exhaled heavily. Was she going to chicken out, or did she have to the guts to stand up for what she believed in? Although he already knew the answer to that question with her show of defiance in the face of adversity earlier in the night, Barry still watched avidly, waiting to see what she would do first.

She surprised him when she leaned over Turner, her arms on either side of his shoulders, and bent down so she could kiss him. Barry had expected her to run her hands over Turner's chest since she was such a tactile person. She hadn't shown that side of herself to them as yet, but he had seen it in the way she touched or brushed up against him as they worked together in the bar, and when he or Turner touched her she would unconsciously arch or press into their touch.

The kiss Charlie bestowed on Turner started off slow. She just pressed her mouth to his and then brushed her lips back and forth. Turner clenched his hands into fists, and Barry knew his friend was having a hard time controlling his dominant tendencies. If and when it was his turn, he hoped he could just lie still and relax, but he was sure he would want to break out of the restraints and take over.

Turner groaned and opened his mouth when Charlie licked over his lips. She whimpered and then thrust her tongue in between Turner's lips and teeth. The kiss turned hot, wet, wild, and carnal. Turner opened his hands and fisted the sheet beneath his body, obviously trying to find an anchor in the fierce storm of passion their little sub was creating.

When she finally pulled back, they were both breathing heavily. Barry was so aroused his cock was moving with every beat of his heart and he didn't know how long he could stay off on the sidelines watching. He wanted to get on the bed, grab hold of Charlie's hips, plunge his cock into her body, and fuck her hard and deep until they both screamed with pleasure.

But he couldn't. They had given control to her, and if they wanted to have another chance with her he was going to have to rein in his libido. He palmed his dick and stroked his fist up and down slowly, trying to relieve the incessant ache, but it didn't help. Moisture seeped from the top of his penis and he reached down to yank on his balls. He was in danger of shooting off and she wasn't even touching him yet.

Then the little minx wiggled her way down the bed. Her ass cheeks flexed and rippled beneath the fabric of her skirt and he groaned with unquenched desire. Charlie turned her head and looked at him. She seemed mesmerized when he gripped his cock again and pumped his hand up and down his shaft. When she lifted her gaze to his, he let her see how hungry he was for her. Charlie turned back to Turner and with feminine grace straddled his thighs.

"Baby, why don't you take your skirt and corset off first?" Turner suggested in a deep rumbling voice.

Charlie gave a nod and scrambled off the bed. Her hands were shaking when she reached for the first hook and eye on her top. It seemed to take forever for her to release the last clasp because he was eager to see her sexy naked body again. Her breasts spilled out and her dusky, rosy-colored nipples were so hard they were standing up in tight little buds. He knew what she tasted like and licked his lips as he remembered how sweet those hard little berries were.

She ran her hands over Turner's chest and down his torso to his abs. Her fingertips followed the outline of his defined abdominal muscles and then traced through the narrow trail of hair which led to his groin. Barry had heard some of the subs in the club call the line of hair on a guy's stomach a treasure trail. Since Turner's cock was rock hard there was no way she could continue on that journey without reaching the treasure.

Charlie was just full of surprises tonight. She didn't hesitate at all. She wrapped her hand around Turner's cock and pumped it a few times. When she released him again, Turner groaned and thrust his hips up.

* * * *

Turner didn't know how much more he could stand. He was so used to being in control he was having a hard time relaxing with restraints around his ankles and wrists. When Charlie palmed his cock, he had to grit his teeth because he was so close to coming his balls had drawn up. Her hand was so much smaller and softer than his, and her grip was much lighter than the one he used when he took himself in hand. But because he needed her touch, loved her, just a brush of her skin against his was enough to have him on edge.

Oh shit! I don't know if I can hold off. I love her so much she has me on edge from just the touch of her hand. I can't wait to feel her mouth on my cock. God, I want her living here with us. I want her in my bed permanently. Will she accept if I ask? Her hands are so soft and gentle, but I want her to sink down over my cock and make love to me, but what would satisfy me more is flipping her over and shoving my dick into her pussy so I can ride her hard and fast until we're both screaming.

He wanted to escape the cuffs, grab hold of her, roll her onto her back, and pin her with his body and fuck her until neither of them could walk, but he had promised that tonight was all hers. Grinding his teeth so hard they ached, he started going through the multiplication tables so he wouldn't embarrass himself.

He jolted when her little wet tongue slid over the top of his dick. He bucked his hips up for more. Whether she was answering his needs or seeing to her own he didn't know, but he growled low in his throat as her lips closed around the head of his cock and sucked him in. As she withdrew, her teeth scraped over his flesh and the sensitive mushroom-shaped head. She laved the underside of his cock and the sensitive spot beneath, which had his erection pulsing in her mouth.

She sucked him back in and took him almost to the back of her throat. His balls were an aching, roiling mass of cum just waiting to be shot out of the tip of his dick.

Turner didn't know how much longer he was going to be able to hold off. His testicles drew up in his scrotum, and he knew he was about to lose his battle with his control. If his hands had been free he would have threaded his fingers into her hair and guided her bobbing head up and down over his cock, but he had no control whatsoever.

"Baby, if you don't pull off now, you're going to get a mouthful," Turner panted.

His little sub surprised him. She cupped his balls in her hand and rolled them as she sucked him down as far as she could. Turner was lost. The muscles in his body were so taut it was a wonder they weren't pushing out of his skin. His body quivered and he thrust his hips up. The tingle near the base of his spine spread around and coalesced at his groin. The warmth stole up his erection, and then he jerked as cum spewed up his shaft and out the end of his dick. He could hear Charlie gulping as she swallowed down every drop of his essence, and the climax seemed to last forever. When she drew her mouth back up over his cock, she licked him clean and then lifted her head.

He'd never seen her look so damn beautiful. Her lips were red and swollen and her eyes were glazed with passion. He wanted to wrap her up in his arms and never let go. When he tried to move he mentally cursed the restraints keeping him from the woman he loved and glanced over toward where Barry was sitting on the sofa stroking his own rock-hard cock.

Charlie patted him on the thigh and then gave him a soft caress. She moved up the bed and flopped down beside him. When her delectable little body draped over his, he sighed with contentment. He wanted to keep her at his side for the rest of his life and to ask her to marry him, but he knew he and Barry had quite a bit of work to do before he could ask her that all-important question.

"Are you going to release me now, baby?"

She sat up quickly, reached for one of the cuffs, undid it, and then glanced over at Barry. "Could you please help me, Mas—Barry?"

"Sure thing, darlin'." Barry helped Charlie undo all the cuffs on his limbs, and as soon as he was free, he pulled her up against his body and held her tight. "Thank you, Charlene."

She giggled. "Shouldn't it be me thanking you? You let me tie you up."

Turner released her and moved back so he could see her face, and then he reached up and held her by placing his hands on both her cheeks. "I would do anything for you, Charlene."

"Really?" she asked breathily.

"Yes, baby. Really." He leaned forward and kissed her nose. "Now, what would you like to do with Barry?"

"Umm, I'm not sure." She tilted her head in contemplation.

"Do you trust me, Charlene?" Turner asked. "Do you believe me when I say I never meant to hurt or humiliate you or make disparaging comments about you?"

"Yes," she finally answered with a sigh. "I know you didn't mean to make me feel bad, but what you said hurt me."

Turner drew her back into his arms and kissed her head. "I know, baby, and I will always regret that I spoke without thinking over what I said first. Please believe me when I say I will never intentionally hurt you. Not ever."

"I do."

"Good. Now will you let Barry and I take over again?"

"Yes!" The tension left Charlie's shoulders. She was obviously relieved to give control back to them.

"Good little sub. Lie down in the middle of the bed on your back," Turner ordered. His woman moved without hesitation and did as she was told.

"Spread those legs, darlin'," Barry demanded as he rose to his feet and walked toward the bed.

Charlie complied with the directive, and then he and Barry secured the cuffs, testing that they weren't too tight by running a finger beneath the lined leather. Turner got on the bed beside her and lay on his side. He cupped her cheek and turned her face toward him and then lowered his head. Turner groaned with appreciation as she opened to him and her sweet feminine flavor of mint and her own unique taste exploded on his taste buds. He swept her mouth with his tongue and explored every nook and cranny he could reach. Her tongue slid along his and she mewled as she arched her chest up, begging for his touch.

Turner withdrew his mouth from hers and caressed his hand up her belly, over her torso, and up to her breasts. He cupped one of her fleshy globes, testing the weight in his palm, and then he bent over and took one of her turgid nipples into his mouth. Since his eyes were open, he was aware of Barry climbing onto the end of the bed and settling between her splayed thighs. He suckled on her nipple strongly as Barry made himself comfortable on his stomach and lowered his head toward her pussy. Her juices were glistening on her thighs and the lips of her pussy. It was Barry's turn with their woman, but Turner wanted to get between her legs and lap up her juices. More than that, he wanted to love her with his best friend. He wanted to have her sandwiched between them as they made love together.

He hoped to get his wish before the night ended, but first they would give their little sub some much-needed attention.

Barry licked through her labia and moaned as he tasted her cream. Turner knew just how she tasted, all spicy and sweet at the same time. He reached over with his free hand and squeezed the nipple of her other breast between his thumb and finger as he sucked on her other peak. She arched up so high she nearly threw him off.

Barry lifted his head. "Hold her down."

He shifted his hand from her breast to her stomach and applied pressure but made sure he didn't hurt her. She cried out with need and frustration when Barry pushed down on her pubic bone and wrapped his arm around one of her thighs. Then he licked her from asshole to clit. Charlie moaned and tried to surge up into their touch, but they held her down.

"Oh God. Please. I need you to touch me. I need more."

"Shh, baby. We'll give you what you need." Turner nipped her earlobe and then licked his way down her throat to the sensitive bit of skin where her shoulder and neck met.

"Oh please," she sobbed. "I can't stand it."

Turner became concerned and lifted his head to look into Charlie's eyes. They were glazed over with passion and a need so great he felt that he could see into the depths of her soul. What he saw there caused his heart to stutter and then beat out a rapid tattoo inside his chest. The love and devotion in her passion-glazed eyes humbled him.

"You are such a beautiful, sexy, passionate woman, Charlene Seward. I love you more than the air I breathe." Turner hadn't realized he was going to say those words until it was too late. He waited with bated breath to see if she would respond.

"Really?" she gasped. "Do you really mean that?"

"I've never meant anything more."

"Oh," she cried as moisture formed in her eyes. "I love you, too. I love you both so much."

Barry lifted his head and wiped her juice from his chin. "I love you, too, honey. God, you don't know how much." He maneuvered up the bed until he was almost blanketing her and kissed her passionately. "Charlie, we want you to stay here with us tonight. Will you do that, honey?"

Charlie smiled and nodded her head. "Yes. I don't want to go home to my empty apartment. I don't know how or why you two are *it* for me, but there you have it."

"We are so glad you love us, baby. We would be lost without you. We want you so much." Turner bussed her lips with his and then drew back again. "Now, it seems our little sub is in need of some attention. Lie back and relax for us, Charlie. We want to make love with you."

"Oh, I can't think of anything I want more."

Charlie settled back on the pillow with a smile and sighed with what he gathered was contentment and joy now that she knew how he and Barry felt about her. He sucked her nipple back into his mouth, suckling strongly as Barry shimmied down the bed and back between her thighs. Between the two of them they had her back on the verge of orgasm within moments. Her breathed hissed out from between her parted lips, and her hips rocked in a rhythm as old as time as Barry licked up and down her pussy and pumped two fingers in and out of her sheath.

Turner released her nipple as Barry lifted up from between her legs, and they undid the restraints and shifted her onto her side. She was facing Barry with her back to Turner, just the way he wanted for what he considered their final claiming of their woman.

He felt humbled by the way she had accepted his apology and vow to never hurt her again. His heart was so full of love and emotion for Charlie and he intended to spend the rest of the night showing her just how much she truly meant to him.

Chapter Ten

Charlie was desperate to have her men inside her. She didn't care where, just as long as they were loving her and touching her. She had never felt so full of love, and the emotions she was feeling were almost overwhelming. The joy that swept through her was close to euphoric, and she needed an outlet or she felt like she was about to burst wide open.

When Master Barry began kissing her, she wrapped her arms around his neck and clung to him. He was an anchor she needed to keep her from floating away into the clouds. She danced a duet with Master Barry's tongue as he slid his along hers and then twirled it around in her mouth. Behind her, Master Turner shifted away for a moment, and then he was back. He kissed along her shoulder and down her back to nibble on a sensitive spot on her shoulder blade. Charlie wriggled her ass and pushed back against him, silently begging for more of his touch. When he parted her butt cheeks and began to massage her anus with cool, wet fingers, she froze.

Master Barry withdrew from her mouth and cupped her cheek. "It's okay, little one. Turner is just getting you ready so we can love you together. Take deep breaths and relax, Charlie."

Charlie whimpered when Master Turner pushed the tip of one finger into her rear entrance. He moved his head close to hers and nibbled on her earlobe. "Don't tense up, baby. Try and stay loose for me. We are going to make you feel so good when we love you together."

She took a deep breath and exhaled slowly, trying to keep her muscles relaxed, but it was so damn hard when her body's instinct was to clench around the invading digit. Master Turner began to ease his finger in and out of her ass slowly, giving her time to adjust to the foreign invasion, and as she relaxed, nerve endings she hadn't known existed began to light up like the Fourth of July. She sobbed as the combination of pleasure and burning pain heightened her lust for more.

"Help her out, Barry," Master Turner demanded in a deep voice.

Master Barry, who had both her nipples between thumbs and fingers, pinching and squeezing them, removed one hand and caressed his way down to her mound. His fingers skimmed over her bare pussy until he reached her wet labia. He parted her lips and stroked from her pussy hole, gathering her cream, and then moved up and gently circled her engorged, aching clit.

"Oh God," she sobbed as more nerves lit up, her pussy and ass clenching as if begging for more. Which they were. The ache inside was so deep it was like nothing she'd ever experienced before.

Master Turner must have added another finger to her ass, because the slight burn got deeper and more intense. She didn't know how much more she could take.

"Please."

"Please what, baby?"

"I need…" she gasped as Master Turner drove deep into her ass.

"What do you need, honey?" Master Barry asked as he flicked her clit, causing her to arch up and cry out.

"You," she panted. "I need you both inside me. *Now!*"

"She's ready," Master Turner growled as he withdrew his fingers from her ass.

"Thank God," Master Barry said through clenched teeth.

He lifted her leg and held it up as he scooted in closer to her. The tip of his cock brushed against her wet pussy, eliciting another groan and gasp from her. And then he was pushing his large penis into her hole. Charlie gripped his shoulders, sighing with delight at the rock-hard muscles moving beneath her hands. They were both handsome, brawny men and they were all hers.

Master Barry surged forward until half his cock was buried in her cunt. Her muscles clenched and released around him, coating him with more of her juices.

"Fuck! You feel so damn good, honey. I never want to leave this little pussy. She's clutching me so tight and I'm not even all the way in yet."

Charlie whimpered, his sexy dirty talk arousing her even more. And then she sighed as he drove into her balls-deep.

"Oh yeah. So good," Master Barry panted. "Hurry the hell up, Turner. I'm not gonna last long."

Master Turner gave her butt a gentle pat and moved back slightly. She heard a squishy wet sound and realized he was lubing his cock up for her. When he moved in close, his front to her back with one arm beneath her head and the other on her hip, she felt surrounded by their love.

"Take a deep breath and let it out for me, baby," Master Turner said, and she did.

As she exhaled, he began to push his way into her ass. The burn intensified, but it felt so damn good, she wanted more. She wanted both her men deep inside her, loving her. When he'd pushed through the first ring of muscle, Master Turner held still, giving her time to get used to having his big, hard cock in her ass, but Charlie wanted him all the way inside. She tensed her muscles and pushed back, whimpering with pleasure as his cock slid along all the sensitive nerve ends.

"Fuck! Don't do that again, Charlie. You could have hurt yourself," Master Turner said in his Dom's voice, but she could hear the emotion underlying his words and again he had slipped up, using her nickname.

Her pussy and ass clamped down on the two cocks embedded in her body at the sound of his deep, controlled voice.

"Oh, I think our little sub liked that. She just clamped down hard and coated me with more of her juices." Master Barry shoved his hips forward, eliciting a moan from her.

"Yeah," Master Turner breathed against her ear, causing her to shiver and goose bumps to erupt all over her skin.

When he pulled back, she moaned, and then the moan turned to a whimper as Master Barry withdrew and Master Turner surged forward again. They eased her into their loving, taking their time and counterthrusting in and out of her pussy and ass. Charlie had never felt so connected, so full of love, or so cherished. With each forward pump of their hips, they picked up the pace until they were sliding their cocks in and out of her body so fast their flesh slapped together.

"Her ass is so fucking tight," Master Turner groaned. "You're gripping me so good, baby."

A slap landed on her ass cheek, and she cried out with pleasure as her insides lit up. Warmth gathered in her womb and traveled down to coalesce in her pussy and throbbing clit. Then the tingling heat gathered in intensity and burned her from the inside out. The coils gathered in closer and closer, preparing to catapult her into the stratosphere. The feelings were so big and intense she began to fight them. But her two Doms weren't about to let her get away with that. Another slap landed on her ass, but this one was much harder and the vibrations sent more pleasure coursing to her pussy and ass.

A hand reached down and a finger caressed over her clit.

"Don't you dare fucking fight us, Charlene!" Master Turner panted in a cold, hard voice. "Let it go, baby. We want it all with you. I love you, Charlie. Come, damn it."

Fingers squeezed her clit firmly and Charlie let go. She hadn't stood a chance in hell of fighting her two dominant men. She threw her head back and screamed. The tension in her muscles snapped, sending her hurtling toward space. Pleasure swamped her. Molten lava traveled outward from her vagina as her pussy and ass clenched and released on the two cocks still shuttling in and out of her body.

White light flashed before her eyes as her body shook, shivered, and trembled. Never had she felt such rapturous pleasure in her life. She was only vaguely aware of first Master Turner yelling and then Master Barry roaring as they reached their own climaxes.

Hands caressed and smoothed over her body as she slowly came back down from her climactic high. Her breath was still ragged and choppy, but as the last shudder left her body, she knew she was where she wanted to be. In between two dominant men who loved her and whom she loved in return. She had finally found a place to belong.

Master Turner shifted behind her and carefully eased from her ass. He gave her bottom a pat and then rose from the bed. Charlie heard water running but was too content and sated to move.

"How do you feel, honey?" Master Barry asked.

"Good," she sighed and finally opened her eyes. Master Barry was smiling at her, and he looked as satisfied as she felt. "I love you, Charlie."

"I love you, too."

The bed dipped behind her and she looked back over her shoulder as Master Turner sat next to her hip. "Let's get you comfortable, little sub."

Master Barry lifted her leg, and they both groaned as he withdrew his softening cock from her pussy. Master Turner cleaned her up with a warm, wet cloth.

"I love you, Charlie. Will you wear our collar again? If you accept our mark of ownership no other Dom would dare to approach you. It would signify our claim on you and you would be under our protection at all times. I would feel much better if you would wear it."

Charlie rolled to her back so she could see both her men. Master Turner's face was an expressionless mask and Master Barry looked tense. *Do they think I am going to deny them?* She decided not to leave them hanging since that was one of the things she wanted most.

"I would be honored to wear your collar and be claimed by you both." She reached up and cupped Turner's face. "I love you so much. I don't want to be without either of you ever again."

"Thank God." Turner nodded at Barry and then leaned down to give her a kiss. This kiss was different from when he had been making love to her. It was passionate, yes, but also full of emotion without the rapacious hunger of before. It was almost…reverent.

When he finally lifted his mouth from hers, he sat near her hip again and smiled at her, love shining from his eyes, just for her. She glanced over to Barry and saw he had the same loving expression on his face. Turner drew her eyes when he began speaking.

"Now that you have accepted us as your Masters we want everyone to know that you are ours. We love you, Charlie." Turner took her hand in his and helped her to sit up. When she was comfortable leaning against the headboard with pillows at her back, Barry drew his hand out from behind his back. He was holding a black box in his large hand.

"Please accept this token as our commitment to you and also our protection."

Charlie took the box when Barry handed it to her and held her breath as she opened it. She gasped when she saw what was inside. Resting on a bed of red velvet lining was a white gold choker with a one-carat diamond in the center, and on either side were two emeralds. Emotion choked her, and even though she wanted to speak, she couldn't. Tears slid down her cheeks and she finally drew in a deep, ragged breath.

"It's beautiful," she rasped. "I will be proud to wear your mark of ownership. Can you please help me put it on?"

Barry took the choker and fastened it around her throat. It was a perfect size. The cool metal nestled against her skin near the base of her neck where her pulse beat rapidly.

She was about to move so she could hug her men but Turner stopped her. "We aren't finished yet, baby." He cleared his throat. "We want you to move in with us, Charlene."

"Yes, we don't want to spend another minute apart from you. Say you'll live here with us." Barry's eyes shone, full of hope.

Charlie hadn't expected this and was flabbergasted. She opened and closed her mouth several times before she could find her voice. "Yes!" It had happened so quickly, but now that she had found her men, her home was wherever they were. Knowing they felt the same way made her heart overflow with emotion.

Barry scooped her up in his arms and pulled her onto his lap. He held her against him and hugged her tight. "Thank you, honey. We will do everything we can to make you happy." He kissed her passionately and then handed her over to Turner.

"You won't regret it, baby. I promise I will never hurt you again. I love you, Charlie."

"Me, too." Charlie wrapped her arms around Turner's neck. He nudged her face up and kissed her long and deep. When he drew back, they were both breathing heavily. Charlie was so happy and full of love, she didn't think she'd be able to sleep. But her two men helped her to settle back down and then slid up close to her. She was surrounded by their warm, hard, muscled bodies. A yawn caught her unaware and her eyelids grew heavy. It seemed she was going to be able to sleep after all.

She nuzzled her nose into Barry's neck and sighed with happiness. Turner was spooning her from behind with his arm snug around her waist. Just as she was drifting off, she heard Turner's deep voice rumbling quietly and felt the vibrations against her back where his chest connected with her.

"Tomorrow you will move in with us, little sub. I'll hire a moving company to come and pack up for you."

Charlie smiled as she let sleep and his bossiness claim her.

* * * *

His patience was finally beginning to pay off. It had taken a few days but he had finally managed to sneak into the club by one of the windows which led to the locker room, off the main foyer. He watched people come and go as he stood in the shadows against the wall and behind a large shrub, which kept him hidden from view.

When it was close to closing he'd slipped into the empty room and found an unoccupied locker. It had been a tight squeeze, but he'd been able to squish into the narrow space and close the door. His head was touching the shelf in the top of the tall metal cupboard and his neck was aching from being cricked at an unnatural angle, but the results would be worth a little pain.

He'd made sure the open window to the room didn't have a sensor alarm attached so he would have an avenue of escape once he had what he wanted. The last thing he needed was to alert the asshole owners that he was on club grounds. The door to the room was slightly ajar and he heard the slamming of the great entrance doors. Not long now. He mentally rubbed his hands together.

She would be his soon, and when he had her in his clutches he intended to show her what it meant to be a real Dom. None of the bastards who came to this club knew complete control over a sub, but he would soon show her what a true Dom was capable of.

The footsteps receded and the internal doors to the great room closed, and then he cautiously left his hiding place. He knew there would be only a small space of time before the alarms were turned on and he had to move quickly. Peeking around the corner of the door, he sighed with relief to see the reception area and foyer empty. He rushed over behind the desk, glanced at the letters on the filing cabinet drawers, and searched until he found what he wanted. After reading the information he placed the file back into the drawer and closed it again. Then he was hurrying back to the locker room. Sweat beaded on his brow as he carefully climbed back through the window and then crouched down behind the bushes. There was a vehicle idling in the parking lot, and he didn't want to be seen by the bright headlights as it drove away.

When the coast was clear, still keeping to the shadows, he hurried down the long drive. He'd parked his car off to the side of the road and it would take him five minutes to reach it. Excitement churned in his belly as he chuckled quietly. She was going to belong to him whether she wanted to or not.

He was just the man to show her what true Domination and submission involved.

Chapter Eleven

As Charlie walked up the footpath toward the front door of her apartment, the hair on her nape prickled and stood on end. She spun around and scanned the area, but there was no one in sight. With a mental shrug she hurried up to her front door and inserted the key into the lock.

As soon as the door closed behind her, Charlie let herself smile. She had spent a wonderful night wrapped up in the arms of two Doms, and this morning they had woken her with caresses and passionate kisses, which had turned to another bout of lovemaking.

Turner had arranged for a moving crew to meet her at her place in an hour, and she had wanted to get to her apartment ahead of time so she could clean out her fridge and pack some of her personal items. She closed the door behind her and dropped her purse onto the counter in the small kitchen as she went about brewing a pot of coffee. While she waited, she began to work, thinking of how old Mr. Jenkins in the apartment next door would benefit from the contents of her small freezer.

As she reached for one of the frozen, wrapped chicken breasts a large hand covered her mouth and nose, and a muscular arm wrapped around her waist. Charlie's scream of fright was muffled by the flesh of his palm.

"Shut the fuck up, you bitch, or I'll knock you out."

Shit! She knew that voice. It was Chad Hilton, the Dom who had been banned from the club. Charlie mentally cursed that she had put her cell phone in her purse instead of her pocket like she usually did. But since she was wearing the skirt and corset from the previous evening, the outfit didn't have any pockets. Barry and Turner had programmed their cell numbers into her phone on speed dial that very morning, and she bemoaned the fact that she wouldn't be able to get to it now that she really needed it and them.

Chad pulled her to her feet and began dragging her across the linoleum floor. He laughed when her hip connected with the wood of the doorjamb but kept right on going toward the front door. Charlie wasn't about to let him drag her outside, because if Chad took her, she was scared she would never see her men again.

The panic that had assailed her began to recede and was replaced with pure, hot anger. She reached up and dug her nails into the hand covering her mouth and the arm around her waist and pulled them down his flesh. She swallowed down the bile threatening to erupt as her nails scored his flesh, digging in with as much force as she could.

He howled with pain and rage, but he let her go. Charlie didn't hang around to look at him. She took off as fast as she could toward her bedroom. She screamed when he grabbed her ponytail and jerked her head back, and she nearly went toppling to the floor on her ass, but she was able to regain her balance as she took two quick steps back. But he was faster, bigger, and so much stronger than she was. He spun her around, and just as she looked up into the evil eyes of Chad Hilton, his fist connected with her jaw.

Pain and stars exploded in front of her eyes and radiated throughout her face, skull, and brain. The breath whooshed from her lungs and her dim world turned upside down when the bastard placed his shoulder into her stomach and lifted her with ease.

A loud pounding sounded in her ears as she fought for breath and tried to remain conscious. As she thought she was about to pass out, she went flying through the air. Although she landed on something soft, the landing sent another fierce knife of pain shooting from her jaw through her head. Her senses were slowly coming back to her, and she realized the pounding had been someone knocking on her door.

The moving guys must have arrived early. She was about to yell out, but the hand covered her mouth again before she was able to get a full breath. The asshole shifted his hand to cover her nose, too. Charlie closed her fist and smashed it into his nose. He cursed viciously and then he hit her again. This time the pain was so intense she lost her battle to stay conscious.

* * * *

Turner glanced at his cell when it rang. Even though the number looked familiar, it wasn't one he had programmed in his phone.

"Hello."

"Mr. Pike?"

"Yes."

"This is Marvin from the moving company. I was wondering when someone will be at the apartment so we can begin packing up."

"Charlene should be there already. Have you knocked on the door?"

"Yes, sir, and quite loudly. My knocking roused one of her elderly neighbors."

Turner began to get a bad feeling in his gut. Charlie should have been at her apartment at least thirty minutes ago. *Keep calm, man. She might have had car trouble.*

"Hang on a second," he said to Marvin and turned toward Barry. "What sort of car does Charlie drive?"

"She drives an old yellow Volkswagen Beetle. What's going on?"

Turner held up his hand and asked Marvin to look around for Charlie's car. "Yes, sir, I see her car. It's parked almost right out front of her apartment, close to the curb."

"I'll be there as fast as I can." Turner disconnected the call and hurried toward the door. "Let's go. Charlie's in trouble."

Barry hadn't even closed the passenger door before Turner slammed his car into gear and planted his foot on the accelerator. His sports car fishtailed down the driveway. When he hit the black tarmac, he floored it, racing through the gears as he explained that Charlie wasn't answering her door.

"Fuck. Do you think she's hurt?"

"I have a really bad feeling about this."

"What? You think someone is out to hurt her? Who would want..." Barry slammed his fist down on the dashboard. "Fucking hell. Chad Hilton."

"That would be my guess. He's the type to blame someone else for his own actions and hold a grudge."

"Hurry the hell up," Barry shouted.

Turner had never been so grateful that he owned a fast sports car than right at this moment. What would have probably taken twenty to thirty minutes to travel at normal speed took him twelve. He pushed his car to the limits, slamming through the gears, weaving and dodging traffic. Even if the cops had shown up, he wouldn't have stopped until he was at Charlie's.

He brought the car to a screeching halt, and Barry was out of the door before he could turn off the engine. Turner ran after Barry as his friend slammed through the front door of Charlie's home. His eyes scanned her small living space as he rushed through her apartment. Barry held up a finger and pointed toward the closed bedroom door. They both listened intently but couldn't hear anything. If Chad Hilton was inside that room with Charlie and they busted through, they could be putting her in harm's way. That asshole could have a gun pointed at her. Turner racked his brain, trying to think of a way to distract the asshole so Barry could get the jump on him and they could keep their love safe.

He motioned to the front door and made a half-circle sign so Barry would understand what he was going to do and at his friend's nod, quietly left the apartment. He made his way toward the back of her apartment, past the kitchen window, and then to her bedroom. Keeping out of sight while he peeked into the bedroom, he almost crumpled with relief when he saw that Hilton wasn't packing.

But when he looked toward Charlie on the bed through the gap in the blinds, white-hot rage filled him. His little sub had a bruise on her face and she looked like she was out cold.

Turner didn't remember much after that as fury consumed him. He was only slightly aware of the tinkling of glass and the crash of the bedroom door slamming against the opposite wall as he reached out for Chad Hilton's throat. He easily blocked the other man's punches with his free hand as he squeezed hard.

Barry grabbed the asshole's arms and pinned them behind his back as Turner tried to crush the life out of the fucker who had hurt his woman. It took him a while to register that Barry was talking to him.

"Turner, he can't get away. You have to let him go or you're gonna kill him. Come on, man, get it together. Charlie needs us."

"Charlie," Turner repeated and finally the red haze which had been covering his eyes receded. He dropped his hand from Hilton and rushed over to his little sub.

He glanced over to Barry as he carefully pulled Charlie into his arms and was in time to see Barry's fist slam into Chad's jaw, knocking the bastard out cold. Barry dropped the asshole to the floor and called 9-1-1.

Ten minutes later, paramedics and cops fought for room in Charlie's small apartment. The medics checked her over, and just as they were loading her onto a stretcher she began to regain consciousness with a moan. They wheeled her out, and Turner didn't hesitate to climb into the back of the ambulance, knowing Barry would deal with the police as well as the moving guys.

Turner watched as the paramedics assessed Charlie, silently cursing that she was hurt. If he or Barry had gone with her this morning, then she wouldn't be suffering now. He felt like he'd failed her yet again. He pushed his guilt aside when Charlie moaned again.

"Shh, baby. You're going to be okay. We're on the way to the hospital, Charlie."

"Turner?"

"Don't talk, baby. You need to rest."

"Love you," Charlie mumbled as she slid back into sleep.

Turner followed the gurney into the examination cubicle and stared the doctor down as he told him to leave. He recognized another Dom when he saw one, but he wasn't about to be pushed around. Charlie needed him close just as much as he needed to be close to her.

"Is she a relation?" the doctor asked.

"She's my girlfriend."

"She'll be fine. There are no lasting effects to the punch she received to the jaw. She will be bruised and sore for a few days as well as suffer from a headache, but that should be it. There are no signs of concussion or fractures. Did you get the asshole that did this?"

"I did."

"Good."

The doctor smiled as Charlie opened her eyes again and blinked a few times. Turner rushed to her side and held her hand.

"Hello, Charlie, I'm Doctor Jason Freemont. Other than the obvious aches and pains, how are you feeling?"

"Tired," she sighed then her eyes grew wider as she stared at the doctor. Turner wondered if his little sub had picked up on the fact the doc was also a Dominant.

"You don't have a concussion." Jason frowned and stepped forward.

Charlie giggled and then winced as the motion hurt her bruised face. "I had a late night. Sir."

"Ah, that explains it." The doctor smiled and winked.

"Where is she? How are you feeling, honey?" Barry almost shoved the doctor aside in order to get to Charlie.

"Two?" Jason raised an eyebrow at Charlie and then turned toward him.

"Yes. Do you have a problem with that?" Charlie asked belligerently.

The doctor gave her a wink and patted her foot. "Not at all, sub. I am, however, a might envious. I want what your Doms have. Take care of her."

After the doctor cared for their woman, Turner shook his hand and passed over a card to his club. "If you're ever in the neighborhood, please feel free to drop in."

Jason glanced down at the card and then smiled. "Maybe I will. Can I bring a guest or two?"

"Sure."

"You can take your sub home as soon as the nurse comes around with the paperwork, but she needs to rest for a few days." The doctor left without a backward glance.

Turner gripped Charlie's hand and brought it up and kissed her knuckles. "I'm sorry, baby. I should have come with you. I feel responsible for your injuries."

"Did you punch me, Turner?"

"No."

"Have you ever hit me in anger or tried to hurt me?"

"You know I haven't, baby."

"You aren't responsible, Turner, so let that guilt go right now."

Turner leaned down and kissed her temple and let the tension drain away, because he knew she was right. It hadn't been his fault.

As he drew back, Barry kissed her head and then began stroking her hair. The two men looked toward the curtain as the nurse entered with Charlie's release forms.

* * * *

Over the next week, Turner and Barry hardly left Charlie's side. They catered to her every need and made sure she did nothing but rest. Turner had called his doctor that morning to give her another once-over just to make sure she was healing well. Apart from the fading bruise on her jaw, she was fine.

As much as she appreciated the way they looked after her, she was becoming sexually frustrated. They treated her like she was made of glass and could break at any moment, and she was tired of being made to feel like an invalid. She had slept in their bed every night, and even though she had tried everything she could think of to get her two men to make love with her, they hadn't taken the bait. She was going to have to do something drastic, because she wanted her Doms back. Fortunately she had an idea of how to get their attention.

She took a quick shower, dried off, and sauntered out to the living room, where her two men were talking quietly. Barry halted midsentence and stared at her naked body. He perused her from head to toe and back up again, stopping at her groin and breasts. Charlie reached up and took her breast in hand and flicked her thumbs over her nipples. She thought she heard a groan, but when she looked from Barry and then to Turner, their faces were free of expression. Well, two or maybe three could play this game.

Lifting her breast up, she lowered her head and licked over her own nipple. Since her head was down she didn't see them move, but one moment she was standing in the living room and the next she was being carried down the hall. She inhaled the delectable clean scent of Master Barry and wrapped her arms around his neck and then licked along the side of his throat and nipped his skin.

"You are in so much trouble, little sub."

"What did I do?" she asked breathlessly.

"You know damn well that any pleasure you get is to be given by us." Master Turner spoke from behind her.

Charlie hid her smile. Her plan had succeeded just as she had expected it to.

"Don't think that you can control us by getting what you want all the time, Charlie." Master Barry lowered her feet to the floor, making sure she was aware of his arousal when he pushed his hips into her belly and let her feel how hard his cock was.

Master Turner stepped forward and placed the cuffs around her wrists. Then he lifted her arms above her head and snapped the restraints to the chain hanging from the ceiling. They had brought her to their private play room, and Charlie glanced around curiously since she'd never been in here before.

"I think our woman needs to learn some restraint." Master Barry walked across to the cupboard against the far wall and opened a door.

Charlie wondered what sort of toys her two Doms intended to use on her. She tried to see what Master Barry pulled from the cupboard, but Master Turner stepped in front of her, blocking her line of sight. She sighed with excited frustration.

"You don't have any control in this room, do you, little sub?"

"No, Master Turner."

"Such a pretty little sub, I can't wait to get my cock inside that sexy little ass."

Charlie pressed her legs together, trying to surreptitiously appease the ache in her pussy and clit, but a sharp slap landed on her ass and she knew she had been busted.

"Who controls your pleasure, sub?" Master Barry asked as he came to stand behind her.

"You and Master Turner do, Sir."

"Remember that and don't try and make yourself come again." Master Barry slapped her other ass cheek. "Do I make myself clear, Charlie?"

"Yes. Sir."

"Good girl."

The slight breeze at her back let her know Master Barry had moved. She wasn't prepared for the flogger and let out a screech as the suede tails connected with her back.

"What is your safe word, sub?" asked Master Turner.

"Red, Master."

"Continue." Master Turner nodded to Master Barry.

The constant swish and thud of the suede tails hitting her skin were so good they sent tingling warmth spreading throughout her whole body. Master Turner ran his hands over her breasts and pinched her nipples to the point of pain before he let off again. She moaned and arched her chest and hips forward and then pushed her ass toward Master Barry as he wielded the flogger.

Charlie could feel herself being drawn closer and closer to the clouds. She felt like she was floating on a soft bed of need and desire, and she wanted her Masters inside her body. She craved their heat surrounding her as they made love to her and sent her to nirvana. Just as she was about to drift up on that cloud, Master Turner thrust two fingers into her pussy and began to finger-fuck her fast and hard.

"We'll let you go into sub-space another time, baby, but we want you too bad to wait. Come now, little sub."

Charlie screamed as her body obeyed Master Turner's demand. Her pussy contracted and released as pleasure washed over her in her climax, cream leaking from her vagina and dripping down her thighs.

"Good girl, Charlie. You are such an obedient little sub." Master Barry undid the cuffs around her wrists and threw them aside. He picked her up and handed her over to Master Turner.

"Wrap your legs around my waist, baby."

She complied and looped her arms around his neck. He then turned her until her back was resting against the wall and surged into her with one strong thrust until he was balls-deep. He pumped his cock in and out of her pussy a few times, and then he carried her over to Master Barry with his dick still embedded deeply inside her.

"Take a deep breath, honey," Master Barry demanded as he massaged cool lube-coated fingers over her puckered hole. Once he'd lubed her up and stretched her out, he removed his fingers from her anus. She heard the pop of a cap being opened and knew Master Barry was coating his cock with the personal gel. "I'm coming in, Charlie."

Charlie looked up into Master Turner's heated gaze and knew she probably looked as hungry and wild as he did. She cupped the back of his neck and pulled his mouth down to hers. As Master Barry gently but firmly worked his hard cock into her ass, she kissed Master Turner with all her pent-up passion. Their tongues slid and danced together as the fire inside her grew to massive proportions. She drew her mouth back from Master Turner's and gasped for air.

"Please, please, please."

"Please what, baby?"

"Fuck me. Please? I need you both." Charlie didn't care how desperate she sounded. She just needed them to love her, now.

"Yes, baby, yes." Turner growled. He and Master Barry withdrew from her ass and pussy at the same time, and then they surged back in together.

Charlie gasped and moaned and tried to rock her hips, but they held her still. Master Barry was gripping her hips from behind and Master Turner was holding on to her waist. They pounded in and out of her body, surging fast and deep. One moment Charlie was groaning as pleasure washed over her and the next she was standing on the precipice. The storm was upon her, ravaging her from the inside out, but instead of being cold and alone she was warm and hot. Her internal muscles rippled and gathered, and she yelled against the intensity of the feelings and pleasure washing over her.

"Yeah, that's it, little sub. Come for us. Come on Turner's cock," Master Barry panted as he surged deeply into her ass.

The storm took her up and over the edge. Her body shook and shuddered, and cream gushed from her cunt, covering Master Turner's cock with her juices. Her two Doms continued to shuttle their cocks in and out of her body, again and again. Just when she thought the last of her climax was going to fade, Master Turner reached down and pinched her clit. Charlie screamed as another orgasm washed over her. She was only vaguely aware of her men's yells as they pumped her back channel and her vagina full of their cum and then everything turned black.

When Charlie became aware once more, she was lying on the bed in Master Turner's room, and he and Master Barry were caressing all over her body.

"Welcome back, baby." Turner kissed her gently on the mouth and then snuggled up to her side.

"Hi, honey. How are you feeling?" Barry asked as he stroked her belly.

"I feel wonderful. Did I go to sleep?"

"You passed out, Charlie. The pleasure was so intense you lost consciousness."

"Wow, I knew you two were good, but I didn't know you were lethal."

"Just remember that the next time you goad your Doms into making love to you."

"Oh I don't know. I think my plan is so much better."

"Little minx." Barry smiled and playfully tapped her on the nose.

"Charlene, you are such a wonderful woman and I love you very much. Would you do me the honor of marrying me tomorrow?" Turner asked in a nonchalant voice and brought out his hand from behind his back.

Charlie stared at the white gold ring with a large emerald nestled in the middle of two smaller diamonds uncomprehendingly for a moment. Then his words echoed in her head. *"Would you do me the honor of marrying me tomorrow?"*

Charlie bolted upright. "What did... Did you just..."

"Take a breath, darlin'," Barry ordered in his Dom voice.

"Are you serious?"

"I have never been more serious in my life, Charlene. We nearly lost you, Charlene, and I couldn't bear not spending every minute of the rest of my life with you."

"But I don't want to cause a rift between you two. How can this work? I can only marry one of you."

"Settle down, honey." Barry sat up and pulled Charlie onto his lap. "Turner and I have already talked this over. He is more prominent in the BDSM community than I am, and we want to make sure you are well taken care of. You will marry him in a ceremony, but in my heart you will belong to me, too. I love you so much, sugar. Nearly losing you made us realize how fragile life truly is. We don't know what the future will hold, but we both know that we want you in our lives permanently. So will you marry us?"

Charlie placed her hand on Barry's cheek. "Are you sure?"

"Yeah, I'm sure, darlin'. As far as I'm concerned we are already married. As soon as you accepted us into your life and had that collar around your throat, you became ours. Nothing would please me more than to see our ring on your finger and for you to become our wife."

Charlie squeezed her arms around Barry's waist and kissed his throat. She looked into his blue eyes and then into Turner's green gaze. "In that case, I would be honored to marry you both tomorrow."

Barry plucked the ring from Turner's hand and slid it onto her ring finger. She didn't know if she imagined it but the white gold felt heated and caused a tingle to travel through her body.

Her men surrounded her with their warmth and the joyful love, and all the emotion inside her bubbled up to the surface. She laughed with happiness as tears streamed down her face.

She had never imagined that she would end up with two handsome, sexy, brawny men, but what woman wouldn't jump at the chance?

Charlie couldn't wait to begin the rest of her life sandwiched between two Doms.

THE END

WWW.BECCAVAN-EROTICROMANCE.COM

ABOUT THE AUTHOR

My name is Becca Van. I live in Australia with my wonderful hubby of many years, as well as my two children.

I read my first romance, which I found in the school library, at the age of thirteen and haven't stopped reading them since. It is so wonderful to know that love is still alive and strong when there seems to be so much conflict in the world.

I dreamed of writing my own book one day but, unfortunately, didn't follow my dream for many years. But once I started I knew writing was what I wanted to continue doing.

I love to escape from the world and curl up with a good romance, to see how the characters unfold and conflict is dealt with. I have read many books and love all facets of the romance genre, from historical to erotic romance. I am a sucker for a happy ending.

For all titles by Becca Van, please visit
www.bookstrand.com/becca-van

Siren Publishing, Inc.
www.SirenPublishing.com

CPSIA information can be obtained at www.ICGtesting.com
Printed in the USA
BVOW03s1156310114

343613BV00012B/103/P